RESCUING ROSIE

Rescuing Rosie

Patricia Buck

Patricia Buck

To order additional copies of this book, contact:
Xlibris
1-888-795-4274
www.Xlibris.com
Orders@Xlibris.com
764201

This book, and *Finding Edgar* are dedicated to the memory of my parents, John and Wilma Rhynard.

ACKNOWLEDGMENTS

I have received so much encouragement on this writing journey. I would love to thank all those who asked me how my book was coming during the long process of writing and finally publishing *Finding Edgar.* This interest has continued with this sequel. So many people over the years have bolstered my confidence simply by being interested. I have decided not to use most of your names, as I might inadvertently omit someone, but please know you all did me a world of good.

So thank you to my high school classmates and friends and your spouses; my former colleagues in the teaching profession; my cherished friends of Ann's Breakfast Club; the faithful members of my former sorority; and all my dear friends at First Christian Church.

My family members have supported my efforts by reading and spreading the word about *Edgar.* They include my husband, Gene, who has always believed in me, my son, Roy, and his fiancé, Rhonda; my daughter and son-in-law, Diane and Bill Daughton; my grandchildren: Rachel and Matt Adamson; Stevi and Eric Sy; and Kurtis and Rachel Buck; Ashlynn Daughton-Hemphill and Daniel Hemphill; Tess, and Bridget Daughton. Ever in my heart are my four greats: Gavin Crolla, Ember and Connor Sy, and Greyson Buck.

I grew up with two brothers, John (Duane) and Zane Rhynard; and three sisters. Marcia Gorton, Judy Stafford, and Anita Milne. Their influence on my life and my writing has been profound. (One learns a lot about life and people from one's siblings.) I also wish to thank my sisters-in-law, Norma and Rene Rhynard and my brother-in law, Darrell Harrington, who so willingly read my book. On both sides of our family, nieces and nephews have been incredibly helpful in advertising *Edgar* on social media, and I appreciate it tremendously. Great-nephew Rodney Wenzel, you deserve a special mention for promoting **Finding Edgar** to both children and adults! Thank you!

Several years ago I began a class at Casper College for writers who wanted to produce a novel, taught by journalist and author, Mary Billiter. Mary was so amazing as she listened to our efforts and made notes on what worked and what didn't. She could hear what was lacking and gave extremely helpful suggestions for improvement. And when Mary felt one was ready to publish a book, she not only encouraged, she pushed a bit. Thank you, and God bless you, Mary Billiter!

After Mary moved to Cheyenne, most of her class formed a group, who continue to write and meet twice a month. Members are facilitated by Nurieh Glasgow. Nurieh and each of you has given me helpful feedback. You have all been extremely empathetic and kind, and I value your friendships.

I have three friends, who have been a part of my life for many years and who seemed to never forget I wanted to write: Carol Rae Jarvis from my high school days; Darroll Woods, a friend of at least 50 years; and Penny Cutts, from my teaching days. Each of you has been a blessing in my life. Thank you.

I would like to also recognize the two illustrators, who have designed covers for my books: Lovely Mae Marzon, *Finding Edgar;* Elenei Rae Pulido, *Rescuing Rosie.*

My sincere appreciation also to all those at Xlibris, who have guided me through this process, especially Gretchen Beal.

CONTENTS

CHAPTER 1

Rosie

Right after Thanksgiving in 1952, heavy snows began falling in the McFarland, North Dakota area in earnest, and we never seemed to get ahead of them. A little snow might melt, but the next snow would be heavier. Some days the farmers had to chain up to get their kids to school. Most of them were used to it. Unless a blizzard raged, school was never cancelled.

I didn't mind the snow. My little brother, Edgar, and I lived with the Clausens now, and we had warm clothing, a very comfortable home, and plenty of good food. Living with the Clausens the past few weeks had given Edgar and me comfort and security. It also gave us the kindness of Mr. and Mrs. Clausen and almost two new siblings in their daughter, Annie, and next-door neighbor, Bobby Merrit. Our big brothers, Albert and George, were living on the Sloven farm, where our father had worked before his death.

Christmas preparations were afoot everywhere. On the second Sunday afternoon in December, Mr. Sloven had loaded Bobby, Annie, Edgar, Albert. George, and me in his big truck bed, which was filled with bales of hay and heavy quilts, and had driven us to the pine covered hills a few miles north of town. He owned some of that land. Most of the trees were too big to fit our houses, but we tramped the hills, our boots crunching in the snow, until we found three perfect-sized ones. By Monday morning each house held a decorated Christmas tree and the pungent smell of pine.

I stood looking at the beautiful Clausen tree a moment and felt something catch in my throat.

"Rosie, we gotta go," Bobby Merritt yelled from the front door. "Walzak is giving a test." Mr. Herman Walzak was the math instructor and the most feared teacher in the school.

"Go ahead," I told Bobby and Annie. "I'll be right behind you." I didn't know why, but for the first time since Edgar and I had moved in with the Clausens, I wanted to be alone. I grabbed my school coat and books and headed down the sidewalk, stepping around icy spots, head down.

Had we had a Christmas tree when Mama was well? There hadn't been one since we moved to McFarland, I was sure of that. Mr. Sloven always gave Dad some bonus money at Christmas, and he'd take us to Bismarck and get us a few new school clothes. He would roast a turkey and make mashed potatoes and gravy and open a can of cranberries. Mrs. Sloven would send a huge plate of candies and cookies home with him, and it got eaten very fast. Our last two Christmases had been like that, and I couldn't remember the ones before Mama got sick.

Mama had liked flowers and green things around. We had made a popcorn chain with cranberries on it, once, and I thought I remembered stringing it around a tree. I wished she could see the trees we'd gotten yesterday. Mama had suffered a severe shock when her parents and three younger sisters were killed in a train-car accident almost three years before. She had never recovered from the shock and had to be hospitalized in Fergus Falls, Minnesota. After that, Dad had brought all of us to McFarland to live, and he had worked for Mr. Sloven.

And then just about two months ago, Dad left us. On the same day Mr. Sloven had to fire Dad because of his drinking, he had received a letter from the hospital saying there was nothing more that could be done for Mama. Dad had taken a pistol down to the wooded area by the creek, north of the little house Mr. Sloven rented for us and shot himself.

I tried not to think about it most of the time, but today I got all the way to the elementary school building, five blocks from the Clausens, before I came back to the present. Miss Graud, the sixth-grade teacher was about to ring the bell, when I pushed open the classroom door. She smiled at me as I put my homework in the basket and sat down behind Jennifer Olsen. My homework was done; my hair was neatly pulled back into a ponytail, and I wore a warm white sweater set and a navy blue skirt with knee socks and saddle shoes. I looked quite different from the girl who hurried to get herself and Edgar fed, lunches packed, Edgar delivered to his sitter, Mrs. Chindler, and myself to school, often late with untidy hair.

All that had changed when the Clausens took Edgar and me in. No longer was I responsible for Edgar, though I still kept an eye on him. The Clausens saw to it we had everything we needed, and Mrs. Clausen made sure my homework was done correctly, and that I looked neat and tidy for school. Everybody doted on Edgar, and he was a constantly happy little boy.

At recess, Jennifer waited for me. A big square of concrete in a protected corner of the playground had been cleared of snow, and to keep warm, we began jump roping and chanting. Jump roping was something I was pretty good at; only now I was surrounded by my classmates, instead of being all alone somewhere. Everyone else laughed as they moved rhythmically, and the ropes slapped the concrete. I kept a smile on my face, but I didn't feel happy at all today.

Finally the bell rang, and the rest of the morning was spent doing math problems. I loved math, and sometimes I thought that was why Mrs. Clausen and I clicked so well. In fact, she'd let me write the receipts for small grocery orders and total them up. At first she'd checked my adding, but only yesterday she'd said to a customer, "Don't worry. Rosie has a head for figures; she'll get it right." Of course the customer had still checked it.

"Yes, Ellie. I don't think you'll have any worries with this one," he said.

Walking home for lunch, Bobby overtook Annie and me. "They're opening the skating pond after school. You got any skates that'll fit Rosie and Edgar?"

"I don't know. Probably—unless Mom gave them to the Olsens."

"I don't want to go this time," I told them, but I didn't know why.

CHAPTER 2

Annie

Of course Bobby got so busy figuring out how we could find skates for everybody, he forgot we were all needed at the Farmers Union. Several orders came in on Mondays, and since the store hadn't been open on Sunday, it was a busy day with customers as well. Mom ladled out hot beef stew for us, and I asked right away about skates for Edgar and Rosie.

"We'll have to see. Your old ones might fit Rosie—maybe Mildred has some old ones Bobbie had, or we may have to order them, or get some in Bismarck. But there's no way any of you can go tonight, anyhow. The whole office is full of orders that came in this morning."

Rosie and Edgar didn't say anything. "Do you think, if we all worked really fast, we could get it done before dark?"

"It gets dark way early, Annie. It's December. Sorry, there just isn't time tonight. Don't worry, there's plenty of winter left, and we'll get skates for Rosie and Edgar as soon as we can." When my father spoke up, I knew skating tonight was out.

Bobby was a bit grumpy as we unloaded boxes that evening. Rosie was extra quiet, but Edgar worked like a trooper and chattered away. "Let's count the cans, Annie."

I really enjoyed Edgar's company, and I'd found out it was fun to teach him things. I handed him a pencil. "Look, each one of these boxes has 12 cans. Write 12 three times right under each other."

"Those are real big numbers, Annie."

"Now look at just the numbers here."

"Just the twos?"

"Yeah. Now count up how many two and two and two are."

"Six."

"Okay, now write it under those twos."

"Now, do I add up the ones here?"

"Yes, and write it down."

"So we got 36 cans?"

"That's right."

"Let's do some more, Annie." By the time we restocked all the canned goods, I'd introduced Edgar to multiplication, and I wanted him to show Rosie.

It was totally dark. Bobby went home to start supper, and Edgar headed to the back room to help Dad flatten boxes. Mom needed me.

"Annie, help Mildred out here. I'm going to run home a minute."

"Where's Rosie?" I asked Mildred Merritt, Bobby's grandmother, who worked at the store.

Mildred took a second. "She said she needed to go home, and she was crying. I don't know what was wrong."

CHAPTER 3

Rosie

All day long Mama had been on my mind. I kept wondering if she would ever get well and strong again. I should have been used to not having Mama. She'd been in the State Hospital at Fergus Falls, Minnesota for almost three years, and I'd only seen her once in all that time. Last summer Dad had taken all of us to visit her. She hadn't really paid any attention to us, except for a tiny smile at Edgar, and just when we were leaving, she had reached up and touched my cheek. Sometimes, I could still feel her fingers on my cheek. In her other hand, she'd held a stack of letters I'd written her.

At the Clausens I had my very own room, and so did Edgar. I loved the pretty curtains and bedspread in a cheery yellow print Mrs. Clausen had hired Mrs. Olsen to make for me, and the comfy warm blankets. Annie and I shared the upstairs bathroom. I liked Annie, and that had surprised me, because she'd never paid any attention to me before.

Today, though, I was overwhelmed with sadness. I had gotten my boxes unpacked, but suddenly I'd known I was going to cry. "I need to go home," I'd told Mrs. Clausen.

She had looked at me. "Okay, Rosie." She was busy with a customer, and I didn't think she'd have noticed my tears.

I took off my skirt and sweater and put on my pajamas and crawled under the blankets, and I cried really hard for the first time since we'd been at the Clausens. I couldn't seem to stop.

So much had happened so quickly. There was the shock of Dad leaving us, which we almost hadn't had time to think about. Everyone had been so kind to us, like Mr. and Mrs. Jim Weisel who lived across the road. They had spent the first night with us, and then after the relatives from Minnesota came, Mrs. Jim had been there with comfort and support, when things really got tough. The sheriff from McFarland had contacted Earl and Ilse Watson, because someone there had thought Earl was Dad's stepbrother. It was Ilse's idea to take my brothers—Albert, George, and Edgar—home with them to live with their five wild boys, and to put me in the state children's home. Mr. and Mrs. Jim and the Clausens, and even Earl tried to talk her out of it, but she was determined. To make matters worse, Albert and George took what money had been put into the sympathy cards, and left in Dad's old truck right after his funeral. They had foolishly broken the speed limit, been rude to the sheriff of the county they were arrested in, and had ended up in a detention center. That meant Old Ilse, as we'd started calling her, was going to take only little Edgar. And no one could talk her out of it.

I had fallen into a deep sleep, exhausted by the turmoil of the last few days. And when I awoke, Edgar was gone—he'd run away in the middle of the night. He was so scared of Old Ilse.

For a little boy of six, he was pretty smart and managed to keep himself well hidden from the search parties that had fanned out from the Weisels. There was some good news that day, though. Mr. Sloven had heard about Dad only after the funeral. There was nothing he could do for Dad, but he immediately went after George and Albert, who had been separated from each other in the detention center and were truly terrified. Having Mr. Sloven rescue them and offer them a home overwhelmed them with gratitude. Their surliness was gone. They were really sorry for deserting Edgar and me, and were determined to find him.

Mr. Sloven had also let Earl and Ilse know they should head back to Minnesota, that the folks of McFarland would be looking after all the Stample kids.

The search had gone on for two days, but on the second day a letter arrived for me that Edgar had mailed from a mailbox on the road that ran by the Dixon farm. That gave us something to go on, and Edgar had been found warm and safe in the old homesteader's house on the Dixon farm.

"Rosie—" Mrs. Clausen came up the stairs. She knocked on my door. "May I come in?"

I blew my nose. "Yes."

"What is it, Rosie? Do you want to tell me?"

"I don't know—I was thinking about the Christmas tree, then I started thinking about Mama. And then I started thinking about Dad, and I got lonesome for them, I guess."

She was quiet for a long time, just sitting there. Finally, she said, "You know I remember when my mother died, and I went to live with my sister. I was twelve, I guess. Sometimes I just needed to go off by myself and cry."

"Did it help?"

'Well, I was calmer afterward. It took awhile to be really happy, but one day I realized I didn't hurt anymore."

"Do you think Mama will ever get well?"

"Rosie, honey, I just don't know. The people at the hospital aren't very hopeful."

"I wonder if I should keep writing letters to her."

"Yes, you should. The nurses always read your letters to her. They say your letters make everyone who reads them, or hears them, feel better. They think your mama hears them."

Mrs. Clausen called the hospital every Monday morning, and she reported back to us what the head nurse had told her. This morning the nurse said Mama had simply shut out the rest of the world. I got up and hung up my skirt and folded my sweater to put away. I put on jeans and a bright green-plaid flannel shirt. Mrs. Clausen gave me a hug and reminded me tonight was Edgar's and my night to eat supper with Mr. and Mrs., Jim.

We always had a good time with Mr. and Mrs. Jim. We had become great friends during the days leading up to Dad's funeral. Mrs. Jim had seen to it that Edgar and I didn't have to be around Isle and the five wild boys. And when Isle said really mean things to me after Edgar ran away, Mrs. Jim had stopped her.

Tonight, as I dried the supper dishes for her and Edgar and Mr. Jim sat up the card table, she took a deep breath. "Rosie, I've got some very exciting news."

"What?"

"Jim and I are having a baby. In June. And I'm gonna want you to come help me sometimes, and when the baby gets big enough, I suppose we'll need a baby sitter once in a while—right now, I can't imagine ever wanting to go anywhere without him –or her. Anyway, I know you'd be a great babysitter. I saw how you looked after Edgar."

I didn't know what to say. I was so happy for her. "Oh. Yes—I'll come anytime."

CHAPTER 4

Annie

On the night that Edgar and Rosie went to the Weisels for supper, my father, mother, and I slipped back into our old routine and sat at our old places. It felt good to be together, just the three of us, but already I looked forward to Edgar and Rosie coming home later in the evening.

"Why was Rosie crying?" I'd decided I might as well find out.

"She misses her parents. The Christmas tree somehow reminded her of her mother. And she's worried her mother won't ever get well."

"What did you tell her?"

"I told her the truth, that I just didn't know, and that the hospital people aren't hopeful."

My father took a sip of coffee. "How do you think all this is working out, Annie?"

"Okay, I guess. Edgar's lots of fun, and Rosie is so—helpful. And nice. She's like Bobby said, just quiet."

He turned to my mother who had begun clearing the table. "Do you think we should take them to see their mother?"

"They—the medical folks—don't recommend it. They say she's changed so much physically, it would be like visiting a stranger,"

I wished they wouldn't talk about Rosie's mother. It was so sad. I wanted to talk about something happy. "I wonder what I should get them for Christmas. I have a little over eight dollars saved, and I was thinking about a toy cash register for Edgar. I could teach him how to make change. And Rosie's been reading my Nancy Drew books so—"

My father looked at the calendar. "Well, it will be a busy time for us. The Merritts are going to Chicago to visit Lydia—so it will just be our family running the Union, and you know somebody always needs gas or food or something on Christmas Day, even if we're closed, so I'd suggest we keep our celebrations pretty simple."

"Well, Santa has to come for Edgar, doesn't he?" I winked at Dad.

"I suppose he does at that."

"I'd like the Slovens to come home with us after church on Christmas Eve, so Rosie and Edgar can be with their brothers for a little while, too." My mother looked at the list she was working on.

"I agree," my father said, "but I'm not sure how simple this will end up being." In fact, none of us could have guessed how complicated Christmas was going to get.

CHAPTER 5

Rosie

Bobby and Annie didn't rest, or let anyone else rest, until a pair of ice skates was found for both Edgar and me. Turned out Bobby's grandmother had saved the first pair he had worn, and they fit Edgar if he put on an extra pair of socks; and Annie's old ones worked for me. I really didn't want to go. For one thing I didn't know how to skate, and I was pretty sure I'd spend most of my time falling down. And truth be told, all I really wanted to do was finish my chores for Mrs. Clausen and whatever job awaited me at the store, and go to bed and cry. Edgar, though, insisted I come, even after I'd talked Bobby and Annie down.

"Just think, Rosie. If you don't come, you'll never learn how, and Bobby and me and Annie will have all the fun."

I didn't feel like having fun, but I knew I should take the chance I'd been given to learn how to skate. I liked being with Edgar and Annie and Bobby and the Olsen kids. Bobby could make anybody laugh, no matter how much a person was sure she'd never feel like laughing again. Annie loved teaching Edgar new things, so it fell to the Olsens and Bobby to instruct me. The funny thing was, that once I got on the ice, my arms and legs and feet knew what to do, and a memory came back to me.

I was six years old, and we were on a small lake in Minnesota. Somehow, Mama and Dad had provided ice skates for all of us. Albert and George could skate on their own and my parents took turns teaching me. Suddenly I was skating across the ice singing "Jingle Bells", and everyone was laughing. Edgar was a year old, and Mom and Dad took turns holding both his little hands and "skating him" in front of them.

Five years had passed, and I still knew how to skate, and for the next hour I flew over the ice, laughing and joining Annie and Evelyn and Elizabeth and Jennifer in a chain, pure joy filling my body. I hoped we could go again soon, maybe on Sunday afternoon. Edgar was having a wonderful time, effortlessly skimming across the pond, as if he'd been doing it all his life.

Walking home, Edgar demanded, "When can we go again, Bobby?" Edgar apparently thought Bobby made all ice-skating decisions.

Bobby had picked up a stick and was pushing the snow off the short bushes we passed. "I can't go again until after Christmas. This is the 17th, and we leave on the early train on the 20th—that's Saturday. I wish my mom would've come here. I never have any fun in Chicago." He kept beating the snow off the bushes. "But you guys can all go."

"It won't be as much fun without you, Bobby."

"We'll still have fun, Edgar." Annie seemed a bit short.

Bobby had brought up another subject I was worried about. It was the 17th. That meant Christmas was eight days away, and Edgar and I had no gifts to give anybody. The Clausens gave all of us an allowance, and I'd saved almost all of mine, but was that enough for gifts for everyone?

Before I went to bed that night, I counted my money: seven dollars and eighty-two cents. Who did I need to buy presents for? My three brothers, Mr and Mrs. Clausen, and Annie. I was almost glad Bobby wouldn't be here, because I couldn't stretch my money any farther. Since the Merritts were leaving town, there'd be no trips to Bismarck for shopping: we'd all be needed at the store. Of course McFarland had a few small stores—a dime store, a drug store, and a hardware store. Would I be able to find anything there? And, I thought Edgar should give everyone a gift, too. I should talk to him about that whenever we were alone. I tossed and turned, and then I thought of someone who would have an idea. I would try to go see her the next day.

CHAPTER 6

Annie

At seven o'clock on the morning of Saturday the 20th, Edgar, Rosie, and I walked down to McFarland's small train depot to watch Bobby and his grandparents set off to Chicago for their Christmas visit with Lydia, Bobby's mother. The plan was they'd arrive home by New Year's Eve.

My father had driven them and their luggage down to the station, so there wasn't really room for the three of us in the car. For some reason, Edgar was very upset he wasn't going to see Bobby off, so my mother suggested Rosie and I walk down with him, as it was only a few blocks and there was plenty of time. Rosie simply put on her coat, and Edgar hurried to his room to "get something important". My mother was on her way to the store, and I stood on the back steps and asked, 'Why do we have to do this?"

"Well, for starters, I asked you to. Also Edgar's never seen anyone off on a trip before, and also because he wants to say good bye to Bobby."

I knew better than to argue, but lately Bobby had annoyed me—always jumping in when I was trying to teach Edgar stuff. You would think it was the Merritts, taking in Rosie and Edgar, instead of us. Bobby always acted as if he was responsible for Rosie and Edgar, that it was up to him to see they had ice skates, almost as if it would be forgotten left up to me and my parents. Always being the good guy, and getting all the attention. I planned to enjoy having Bobby gone for all it was worth.

It was a cold morning, and the few passengers waited in the station, not on the platform as they sometimes did in the summer. Bobby was dressed in dark blue corduroy pants, red striped sweater, and brown loafers. He was carrying his gray wool jacket, and some part of my brain thought he looked reasonably neat, and I was even, for just one second, halfway proud that he was my best friend. Mr. and Mrs. Merritt wore their Sunday clothes. She stood checking their tickets; he was talking to my dad, like he was trying to be certain he hadn't forgotten anything.

Edgar rushed to Bobby. "Hey! Bobby! We came to see you off!"

"Well you got five minutes—they just announced it."

Edgar reached into his coat pocket and handed Bobby a package. I had no idea what was in it. "Thanks, Edgar." Bobby patted his shoulder.

Rosie fidgeted with her coat buttons. "Hope you have a good time, Bobby."

Edgar pulled on Bobby's hands. "I'll miss you, Bobby."

I couldn't think of much to say. I'd already decided I wouldn't miss him, and truth be told, I didn't care if he had a good time or not, though I didn't exactly want him to have a bad time. "Tell your mother hello for me—and Merry Christmas to all of you."

"Yes, Merry Christmas to you guys, too." The adults echoed the sentiment as the train whistle drowned all of us out. We stood on the platform behind them. "Bye, Edgar. Bye Rosie. Bye Annie"

"Bye, Bobby," I answered, and he was gone.

It was a busy Saturday, but my parents said they could manage by themselves from two to four, if we wanted to go downtown and Christmas shop a little. We all got our allowances, and bundled up for the walk downtown. It wasn't very far, but it was only about ten degrees.

Rosie held back a little. "I need to go see Mrs. Jim. Can Edgar go shopping with you?"

"Sure. Come on, Edgar." This would be fun. I could help him find gifts for everyone and maybe get them wrapped before Rosie got home. She took off on a run toward the edge of town.

Shopping with Edgar proved way easy. He knew exactly what he wanted to get everyone. "Do you have enough money?"

"Yep. I already added it up." Mom had taken him on a looking trip to the dime store earlier in the week. A bright red fountain pen for Mom, three sturdy flashlights for Dad, Albert, and George, and a box of light yellow stationery for Rosie.

"And yours is a secret, Annie."

I decided I'd shop on Monday, and we rushed home to wrap his presents. I knew where Mom kept boxes and wrapping paper, and it was fun helping Edgar wrap the gifts.

I was surprised by my mother's voice. "Annie, it's a quarter after four. You're needed at the store. You, too, Edgar. Where's Rosie?"

"She went to see Mrs. Jim."

"Well, she knew she needed to be back by four, too." My mother wasn't very pleased with any of us.

CHAPTER 7

Rosie

I had been lucky enough to see Mrs. Jim at the Union the day after our ice skating expedition, the day Bobby had reminded us how little time there was left until Christmas. I was stocking a shelf in the back of the store, when I heard her cheerful, "Hi, Rosie."

I managed to tell her of my dilemma with Christmas presents, and asked for her advice. She thought a moment and said, "Can you come down on Saturday?"

"I don't know. I'll try if the store isn't too busy."

"I've got sort of an idea," she said. "Do you have any money?"

"A little—eight dollars or so."

"Well, can you meet me at the dime store after school tomorrow?"

I wasn't sure I could, but I promised I'd be there. And I'd gone. She was back in the fabric section, when I found her. "I can help you make a pretty apron for Ellie. You could get Annie and your brothers and Mr. Clausen jig saw puzzles. Everybody loves those in the winter." It sounded like a good idea. I picked out a bright green checked cotton for Mrs. Clausen, and chose five interesting looking jigsaws. "I'll get the apron cut out, and we'll sew like crazy when you come on Saturday."

I sneaked the puzzles into the house, before I hurried to the store. Maybe, because it was the time of keeping secrets, nobody asked why I was a few minutes late.

While Annie and Edgar shopped at Ben Franklin's, I ran almost all the way to Mrs. Jim's. Sewing was a skill I didn't have, but Mrs. Jim showed me an easy hemstitch, and I tried my best. She had done the machine sewing and began cross-stitching the pocket. We both worked as quickly as we could, but when we were finally finished and looked at the clock, it was nearly four. "I can't drive you, Rosie. Jim took the car to get it worked on yesterday, and 'course he's got the truck at work."

It had begun to snow a little and was colder, but it wasn't quite dark, and I ran as fast as I could, wearing boots and carrying a bag. Even so, it was nearly 4:30 when I'd hid the apron in my room and hurried to the store. Mrs. Clausen was in the office doing the books, and Mr. Clausen and Annie were managing the customers and the gas pump.

"I'm sorry I'm late," I managed to say before Edgar sat me straight.

"You're in big trouble, Rosie."

Mr. Clausen looked up from the receipt he was writing. "Rosie will you fill the bread racks, please?"

I got busy with the bread; then I unpacked canned goods, and shelved cookies. We took turns going home for supper. Mr. Clausen and Annie took Edgar with them, and since there were few customers by then, I wrote the receipts, while Mrs. Clausen did office work and pumped gas for one customer.

Mrs. Clausen had said we'd make do with meat loaf sandwiches for supper, and she sat mine in front of me along with a glass of milk and a dish of canned peaches. "Rosie, I need to talk to you about a rule we have in this family. I'm very strict about it. If I say four o'clock, I mean four o'clock. I was very worried about you. Please keep this rule in mind. Now, let's eat."

I had a lump in my throat. "I'm sorry."

"I'm sure you are. Just remember the next time."

I hated having Mrs. Clausen get after me, but it had been for her. Maybe, though, what made me feel worse, was the fact she had been worried about me.

CHAPTER 8

Annie

We were out of school for Christmas vacation, and my mother seemed to have a dozen jobs a day for Rosie and me. She loved to bake and so did Rosie, and Edgar and I joined in decorating cookies, and later, packing them into coffee cans to take to some of the townsfolk. We were sent out to deliver cookies on Tuesday the 23rd to the oldest residents of McFarland. We tied an apple crate to the sled and loaded it with the gifts. It was warmer than it had been, and we didn't feel rushed to get out of the cold. The recipients said nice things about how kind it was of my mother to send them cookies. Edgar told everyone that "Rosie and Miz Clausen made them, and Annie and me colored 'em." A few people asked how I liked having a little brother.

"Edgar's lots of fun," I answered truthfully. I didn't want to say anything about him being my brother. His mother might get well and take Edgar and Rosie back to Minnesota, for all I knew, though the conversations Mom had had with the nurse in Fergus Falls sure didn't sound like that was going to happen.

My mother always sent cookies to the Olsens, because Mrs. Olsen rarely had time to do a lot of extra baking, and the children loved the bright frosted Christmas cookies. Evelyn and Elizabeth were both ironing, but they stopped to pour glasses of milk and eat a cookie with their younger siblings and us. "Did you go see Bobby off on the train, Edgar?" Elizabeth was quite interested in Bobby these days, and I couldn't figure out why that annoyed me.

"Yeah. It's not as fun when Bobby's gone."

"Well, I think it's more fun!" I announced.

Evelyn licked at the frosting on her cookie. "Bobby *is* a nice boy."

"I suppose—if you like show-offs," I answered, wishing I hadn't said it before the words were out of my mouth.

"I think he's Annie's boyfriend," Edgar said, a sly little smile working at his lips.

"He certainly is not! It's enough trouble having Bobby Merritt for a friend. Don't ever say that again, Edgar!" I saw Elizabeth wink at Evelyn.

At home Rosie was washing up a few dishes and waiting for a pie to finish baking. "You and Edgar are suppose to go to the store right away. It's awfully busy."

"Do you mind to pump gas this afternoon, Annie? Probably need to change your coat and get some old gloves." I didn't mind, and I knew my dad wasn't really asking a question. I sort of liked pumping gas. I was doing a job, without supervision, that most girls didn't get to do. It was cold out, but I went in and out so much making change for the customers that I wasn't chilled.

I was glad I'd gotten my Christmas shopping done yesterday morning. The hardware store stocked a few toys, and I'd found the cash register I wanted for Edgar, and the Nancy Drew books I'd ordered for Rosie had arrived in the mail. I bought two decks of cards for Albert and George. I had found gifts for my parents last summer in Bismarck at a sidewalk sale: two bright red ceramic coffee mugs bearing the words Mom and Dad. I had filled them full of peppermints. Now, all was ready, and tomorrow was Christmas Eve.

I wondered what Bobby and his grandparents were doing. Surely in a big city like Chicago, you could do lots of fun things—shop in huge department stores, go to movies, eat at fancy restaurants, go ice skating at a real skating rink. I stamped my feet, angry at myself for thinking about Bobby Merritt.

The customer was saying something about a bad storm coming. He was driving to Williston, and he didn't want to run into it, but just in case, he was going to keep that tank topped off.

CHAPTER 9

Rosie

Mrs. Clausen had made her phone call to Fergus Falls, a day late, while Edgar and Annie were out delivering cookies. She didn't say anything for quite awhile and seemed deep in thought. Finally I asked, "How is Mama?"

"She hasn't changed much, Rosie, since last week."

"Do you know if she got my letter?"

"Yes, Rosie, and the nurse said that, when she read it, your mama smiled a little. But that was the last time she's shown any sign of noticing what is going on around her."

"I'll write her another one right away." And I did, telling her all about remembering skating, and how I still could, and how good Edgar was at it. I told her about the Christmas present Mrs. Jim and I had made, and I enclosed a pretty pink handkerchief I'd found for Mama's gift. I told her about baking cookies and Edgar helping to frost them.

I put the letter in the big mailbox on the corner of the street and hurried to help Mrs. Clausen.

By Wednesday, there were lots of packages under the tree. Annie and Edgar were constantly looking under it, checking to see if anything had been added. Albert and George dropped by with several gifts and then grocery shopped for Mrs. Sloven. Edgar and I tagged along behind them. I reported what Mrs. Clausen had found out about Mama. Albert and

George wrote to her, too, now. Mr. Sloven made the same weekly phone call that Mrs. Clausen did, and after he'd heard that Mama seemed to hear my letters, he insisted George and Albert write to her, too.

"You're coming tonight after church, aren't you?"

"Unless it storms."

By 6:00 it had snowed for two hours, and it was clear George and Albert and the Slovens wouldn't be coming. Mr. Clausen made another decision. "I think we'd better skip the Christmas Eve service. The highway is treacherous. Lots of folks are looking for a place to spend the night and get food, and some need gas. I think we need to keep the Union open." He hurried back to the store.

We helped Mrs. Clausen carry our Christmas Eve supper to her small office at the store and made a second trip for soup bowls and spoons. We took turns eating our soup, and munched on cheese and crackers in between customers. "At least we're all together tonight, instead of half of us at home," Mrs. Clausen noted.

By eight o'clock a good six inches of snow blanketed McFarland, and more was falling. One stranger after another appeared, most no longer looking for gas, but for a place to stay the night. The small hotel was full, with even some cots in the lobby. Mrs. Clausen began phoning people. She knew everyone in town who might have a spare room and be willing to offer shelter to a stranger. Mrs. Olsen called to say that the Baptist church basement was available. They had a few cots and lots of blankets.

Mr. Clausen took several packages of lunchmeat out of the cooler and three big loaves of bread from the rack. "Annie, you and Rosie go make up some sandwiches. Take Edgar home, and get him into bed."

"I think you kids better all camp out in the living room," Mrs. Clausen said. "You know where all the extra bedding is, Annie. Use those old quilts, and make yourself beds on the floor. And then change the sheets in your rooms and Edgar's. I think our house will be a hotel tonight."

I made sandwiches, and Annie made beds. I thought how lucky people would be to find a place like the Clausens—food and soft warm beds, and kind people, willing to share. I made 20 sandwiches and cut them neatly. I wasn't sure if it would be needed, but I boiled a kettle of water for tea and started a pot of coffee. "Annie," I yelled up the stairs, "should I take these back to the store?"

I needn't have asked, for at that moment, Mrs. Clausen appeared with a very tired looking family. A man, whose eyes were red from peering at the road, and a woman carrying a tiny baby. "Sandwiches ready, Rosie?"

"Yes."

She sat the tray on the table, along with chips and pickles and a plate of cookies. They eagerly accepted the cups of tea, and the woman asked if she could warm a bottle.

Annie appeared. She had changed all the beds and gotten Edgar to lie down on the living room floor with his Teddy. His room would be used for this couple. They didn't talk very much but thanked Mrs. Clausen over and over for her hospitality. They were from Oregon, on their way to Minneapolis, to show off their new baby.

An elderly couple appeared next. They weren't hungry, but gratefully drank the coffee I poured. Mrs. Clausen led them up to Annie's room. They were on their way to visit their daughter in Williston. Their son, who was driving them, had gone to the Baptist Church to spend the night.

Finally, at midnight Mr. Clausen came home, along with a tall black woman and her little granddaughter from Chicago, who were traveling to Seattle. He introduced them to us as Mrs. Adams and Judy. They would be escorted to my room and seemed especially grateful. "I was sure we'd have to spend the night in the car," the woman said.

Though she said they'd had food with them, they especially enjoyed the sandwiches. Mr. Clausen said the highway was officially closed, and he had locked up the store. "You girls better try and get some sleep."

Annie whispered something to her father, but he only said, "Get some sleep, Annie."

We crawled between the quilts she'd piled on the floor. "This is the strangest Christmas Eve I've ever spent," she said. "It's exciting, though, isn't it?"

In a funny sort of way, it was.

CHAPTER 10

Annie

Trying to sleep on Christmas Eve had always been hard for me. I loved finally waking on Christmas morning for a joyous celebration. Usually it was just Mom and Dad and me wrapped in our robes and blankets, opening our presents, thanking each other. We'd eat a special Christmas breakfast and then settle down to enjoy the gifts, read the new books, eat a few chocolates from the box the Merritts always gave us. The Merritts nearly always spent Christmas with Bobby's mother, Lydia, in Chicago, or she would come to McFarland. When she came, though, we didn't see much of the Merritts. Lydia didn't go out much in McFarland, and though her parents worked their regular shifts at the Union, Bobby tended to spend most of his time with his mother. Still, up until this year, I'd always gotten him something—a book of tricks or jokes or some gadget or other he'd told me about. This year, though, I hadn't bothered, and now I wondered why. I also wondered why I kept thinking about him, when he annoyed me so much.

The blankets and quilts I snuggled under were warm, but the house was a little cold. It was strange to me, listening to Edgar snuffle a bit and almost snore. I'd never really heard anyone else sleep before. Rosie slept like she did everything else, quietly.

I wondered if, somehow, with all these people sheltered here, Santa would be able to come. I wondered if the Olsen kids would wake to new toys, or would their gifts be new coats and jackets their mother had made.

Would Albert and George get expensive new things from the Slovens? Why was I thinking about all this?

What would happen tomorrow with our house full of strangers? I turned on my side and mentally recited all the Christmas hymns and songs and poems I knew. In the middle of *Good King Wenceslas*, I finally fell asleep.

Once, in the night, or maybe it was already early morning, I thought I sensed someone in the living room. I must have stirred a bit. It was only Dad. "Go back to sleep, Annie. I'm just adjusting the furnace—the house is really cold."

As I drifted back to sleep, I heard him descend the basement stairs.

The next time I awoke my mother was calling all of us. "Annie, Rosie, Edgar—hurry and get dressed and put the quilts away. Our guests will be up soon."

It doesn't take long to get dressed when you've slept in most of your clothes. With all the people in the house, we rushed through the bathroom. The house was warmer. My parents motioned for us to come back into the living room. I hadn't noticed that the tree was covered with a large blanket on one side. My father pulled the blanket away to reveal some unwrapped gifts—a box with a farm set for Edgar, a chemistry set for me, and an adding machine for Rosie. And a new pair of ice skates for each of us.

"I guess a snowstorm can shut down the highway, but it doesn't scare Santa any," my dad said.

"Oh, thank you." Already, Rosie's fingers were punching in numbers, and Edgar had gone slightly behind the tree to open the box. I found the instruction manual to the chemistry set and tried to decide where to start.

"Thanks, Mom and Dad."

Edgar came out from behind the tree. "Wow, come look at all my animals, Rosie. And you, too, Annie, and Mr. Clausen and Miz Clausen."

Dad got down on the floor with Edgar and helped him build the barn. Mom went back to the kitchen and started a pot of coffee and heated water for tea. She sat out a big pan of cinnamon rolls and opened three large jars of peaches she'd canned last summer.

"If you kids will all agree, I'm thinking we should wait until Albert and George can be here to open the other gifts."

The guests began to appear, bleary eyed but attempting to be cheerful, the adults saying "Merry Christmas," and everyone enjoying Mom's cinnamon rolls and coffee or tea. They looked out the windows at the whiteness of a blizzard, and took a deep breath. Mrs. Adams asked my mother if she could "borrow our Christmas tree,' and placed a baby doll in a tiny buggy under it. Then she carried her little granddaughter into the room. We all wanted to watch Judy find her gift, but my parents suggested we'd better have a bite of breakfast ourselves.

It was a Christmas Day none of us would ever forget. The wind did not let up, but as the snow swirled around our house, the spirit of Christmas swirled within. The women helped my mother prepare Christmas dinner, breaking bread for stuffing, basting the turkey, peeling the potatoes, making a fruit salad. Rosie held the young couple's baby while the young mother and I sat the table. The little girl pushed her doll in the buggy and visited Edgar at his farm.

The men tried to clear snow away from the doorway. They followed the rope my father kept tied from our back door to the back door of the store. The cars were parked in front of the store, and articles the families needed were retrieved from store, after they fought the blowing snow and managed to get car doors open.

As we sat at the table, the older woman began to talk about what a lovely Christmas we were having. "Once before, I had Christmas with a group of strangers," she said. "We were just married and living in New York—"

"And I had to work all Christmas Day," her husband remembered. "You were all alone."

"Well, I was, until our next door neighbor lady heard me crying—the walls were paper thin in those apartments. She knocked on my door and begged me to come eat Christmas dinner with her and her children. I was timid about it—I didn't know them at all. But I went, and I was always glad I did. Turned out, she was just as lonesome as I was for a woman to talk to. We still write to each other. That was in 1910—forty-two years ago now."

"Strange, isn't it?" my mother conjectured. "Life puts us in all sorts of places and introduces us to people we never expect to meet."

I was watching Rosie, almost nodding. It was true. Here we were together. Last year, if anyone had told me Rosie and Edgar would be part of my family, I would have been sure they were crazy. Rosie was probably thinking the same thing.

By the next morning, you could hear the snow plows clearing the streets and roads, but it would be well into the afternoon before our guests could finally get back on the road. My mother had written down all of their addresses. She hugged Mrs. Adams good-bye, and Rosie and I hugged the little girl. She hugged Edgar. My mother and Mrs. Adams corresponded for years, and she stopped several times to visit on her trips to Seattle. She always referred to my parents as her "angels in the storm".

CHAPTER 11

Rosie

Christmas had come with such a flurry of busyness, I think I would have been sad, if it had been completely over, but since we'd saved our presents for when Albert and George and the Slovens could be there, I still had something to look forward to.

The snowstorm that had locked us in left McFarland with plenty of drifts and piles of snow to be shoveled, and Edgar and Annie and I had our share of it. Edgar loved it. Mr. Clausen had found a little shovel just his size, and Edgar happily went to work. On Saturday, December 27th, the trucks that had been stalled by the storm brought a large stock of groceries and other items. The gas truck came to fill the underground tank, and for several hours everyone was busy. Edgar loved filling the bottom shelves, counting the cans or boxes or jars. I filled racks and flattened boxes and candled eggs and thought a lot about Mama. Had she gotten my letter? Had she enjoyed Christmas at all?

About four o'clock, Annie approached her mother. "Can we have our allowances and go downtown? Everything is unpacked and shelved and there aren't many customers now." The town folk had already shopped, and the country roads hadn't all been cleared yet. Most Saturdays we headed to the matinee at the movie theater, but it was too late for that. I knew Annie wanted to meet the Olsens at the drugstore for a treat, and that the moment her mother agreed, she would be on the phone to Elizabeth or Evelyn.

"Yes, you may. You've all worked like troopers. Dad and I'll take over. But be back by five-thirty." I made a very strong note of that, and Annie hurried to call the Olsens. I hoped Jennifer would come. She was very kind, and slowly we were becoming friends.

Five Olsens were seated at the big round booth across from the soda fountain. They all sported bright new wool jackets. Their mother had been busy. We ordered our cokes and joined them. Jennifer was glad to see me, and Tommy and Timmy and Edgar gabbed away about Christmas and coming to see Edgar's new farm set. Jennifer had brought a Nancy Drew book to lend me. "Have you gotten all the homework done?"

"Yes. Mrs. Clausen got us busy on that the first night." It was true. She said we'd enjoy our vacation more, if we got the homework out of the way.

"When does Bobby get back?" Evelyn asked Annie.

"They said by New Years Eve—I don't know." There was a hint of annoyance in Annie's voice.

"I hope they'll have the ice pond cleared off by then. Billy and Bobby and all of us can go skating again."

"We've all got skates now," said Elizabeth. "It's going to be fun."

"I think we should go just as soon as it's cleared off," Annie said. "We don't have to wait around for Bobby."

CHAPTER 12

Annie

Sunday morning we filed into our pew, rattling Sunday School pamphlets, and settling ourselves for an hour long service. Rosie sat at the farthest end, next to the wall beside Edgar, then my mother, my father and me. You would have thought Rosie and Edgar had attended Sunday services all their lives, as quiet and well behaved as they were. My mother had explained our tithing practice to them, and each Sunday the coin was ready in their pocket. Though Edgar had gotten very self-confident and independent, in church he always leaned on Rosie and often held her hand.

At home we changed into our jeans and sweaters as fast as we could, and had barely got downstairs when the doorbell rang.

Bobby came bursting through the door, and Edgar threw himself headlong into him. "Oh, I'm glad you're home!"

"Hi, Bobby." Rosie looked glad to have him back, too.

"Oh, hi." I kept right on tying my shoes

"We came home early. Mom got called back to work, and Grandpa was worried about the store and all, with the bad weather."

"Did you have fun?" I asked him.

"It was good to see Mom, and we had one day downtown. We shopped in the morning, which Grandma and Mom enjoyed. Stowed our stuff in a locker, and grabbed a sandwich, and went to see "Ben Hur.'

Then we went out to dinner in a pretty good place to eat. Otherwise we just stayed close to Mom's apartment. Played a lot of card games. What about you guys?"

"We had a hotel here, Bobby. You shoulda been here. Want to see my farm?" Edgar pulled on Bobby's hands, but Bobby wasn't through talking to me.

"Is the snow cleaned off the pond yet?"

"Not yet. They've been too busy clearing streets."

"We oughta get a bunch of us together and do it ourselves. The Olsens, us, Zack Jones, some of the other kids. We could do it this afternoon. Sundays are boring anyway. I'm gonna ask your dad and Grandpa. Why don't you call the Olsens?"

He hadn't been back ten minutes, and here he was, hatching up a scheme and pulling me right into it. In less than an hour a dozen town kids with shovels were clearing the snow off the pond. The snow had settled a little, and even small scoops full were heavy. Before long, my dad and Mr. Olsen and Mr. Jones brought their shovels and joined us. By four o'clock, the pond was clear. "Looks like we'll have a full moon tonight," my dad said. "Go on home, and get warmed up, and all of you come back tonight to skate."

My mother had hot chocolate ready for us, and she insisted we lay our mittens and socks on the rack she'd placed above the floor grate to dry out. She was boiling hot dogs for supper, and she had me open a can of pork 'n beans."

By the time we got back to the pond, the moon was coming up. I watched Rosie, who seemed to skate as easily as she walked. She looked very happy in the moonlight. We made chains of ourselves; we skated alone and together. Edgar tugged at my hand and I twirled him around which got him to laughing. Evelyn, Elizabeth, Jennifer, Rosie and I clasped hands and formed a line, then "snapped off the two skaters on the ends. The two discarded players broke through the line and formed a new middle. It was a game we improved upon each time. The boys worked on their speed and skated at the edge of the pond, racing each other. A siren went off at eight o'clock, the time we'd been told to come home. The matter of taking off skates and putting on cold boots was the only unpleasant part of the whole evening.

Edgar was tired, and I saw him grab Rosie's hand. They trotted ahead, and Bobby came up beside me. "That was fun," I said.

"Yeah. I wish Mom would move here. I like this sleepy little place a lot better than Chicago."

It's not sleepy when you're around, I thought, but of course, I didn't say so. Maybe I'd missed him a little after all.

CHAPTER 13

Rosie

On New Year's Eve, the Slovens came with Albert and George. All day Mrs. Clausen and Annie and I had taken turns at the store and turns in the kitchen. There was a wonderful beef roast, mashed potatoes, brown gravy, a fruit salad, green beans, and beautiful, fresh-baked dinner rolls. There was a chocolate pie and a lemon pie with meringue piled high on top of each, compliments of Mrs. Sloven, and a cake decorated with red and white peppermints that was mostly my work. Edgar had made name cards for each place, and Annie had set the table. The Merritts had insisted on running the store. As soon as we'd eaten, Edgar sidled around to Mr. Clausen. "Isn't it time to open presents?"

Mr. Clausen smiled. "I think so, Edgar. You've waited a long time and been a good boy about it."

Annie and I passed out the gifts, and we took turns opening them, wrapping paper piling up around us, as we oohed and aahed. I was happy to have more Nancy Drew books to read, and Edgar was delighted with his cash register. Annie and all the boys were tickled to have a new jigsaw to do. I watched Mrs. Clausen when she opened the apron Mrs. Jim and I had made for her. Her eyes filled with tears. "Oh, Rosie. It's so pretty. How did you ---?"

"Mrs. Jim helped me."

"And that's why you were late that day." She came over and gave me a hug.

Albert and George had brought both Edgar and me sweaters, knitted in a red and white geometric design. We both hugged them, maybe embarrassing them a bit.

We cleaned up the debris, and Annie posed the question we'd all been wondering about. "Can we go skating until the siren goes off?"

Albert and George had brought their skates, and Edgar and Mr. Clausen went to get Bobby. The Merritts would be joining the other adults for cards, and all the kids could skate. The weather was fine tonight, so the Slovens didn't have to rush their leavetaking. "Be sure to work up an appetite," Mrs. Sloven told us. "There's lots of dessert."

We found Zach Jones and the Olsens already at the pond. I loved skating alone and with the other kids. Edgar and the young Olsen boys soon had a "Crack the Whip" game going, and Jennifer and I skated along together. Elizabeth and Annie started singing "Good Night Irene" and we all joined in. I had never felt lighter or freer or more joyful. Bobby suggested we all make a big circle and go out to the edge as far as we could, then come together in the center and back out. Somebody started "Jingle Bells." I was sure this was an evening I'd remember forever.

Walking back to the Clausens, between Albert and George, I asked them how their Christmas had been. "Pretty good, really, but we missed you and Edgar. After we got the chores done and were sure the livestock was safe, we played games, and ate lots of Mrs. Sloven's good cooking. She told us this was the best Christmas they'd had since their son was killed."

The grown ups were deeply engrossed in their game, but as soon as they came to a stopping point, dessert was served. I wanted to try both pies and my cake, and Mrs. Sloven cut me a thin slice of each.

The grown ups went back to their game, and Bobby, Annie, Albert, George, and I started a game of dominoes. Edgar lay on the sofa playing with the paper money and the cash register Annie had given him, but he was worn out from all the skating and cold, fresh air and soon fell asleep.

A little before midnight, the grown ups jokingly called an end to their game, the men sure the women were in cahoots because they'd won. Mr. Clausen turned on the radio just as "Auld Lang Syne" came on. The men kissed their wives, and everyone wished the others Happy New Year.

Mr. Sloven stood. "Well, it's been a wonderful evening, ladies winning notwithstanding, but I think we'd better head for home."

Albert and George hugged me. "See you on Sunday, Rosie. See you, Annie."

Bobby gravely shook hands with everyone. "You all have a wonderful 1953," he said. I could never tell with Bobby, if he was pretending to be a grown up and sort of making fun of their seriousness, or if he was really serious. At that moment, I had no way of knowing that 1953 would not start out wonderful for the Stample kids at all.

CHAPTER 14

Rosie

In all the years I lived in the Clausen house, January 1, 1953 was the only time I was ever awakened by the phone. My bedroom was at the back of the house on the second floor. The only phone was downstairs in the front hallway, positioned there so Mr. and Mrs. Clausen could hear it from their bedroom. Yet, I heard it clearly that morning, and a jolt of dread and resignation went through me. And before it had stopped ringing, Edgar pushed open my door and crawled into bed beside me, his eyes wide and frightened.

We heard the yawning voice of Mrs. Clausen answering the phone. Since it was a holiday, the store was closed. A sign had been posted on the front door to contact the Merritts in case of emergency. The Clausens were getting a well-deserved rest. Her words were indistinct, but after she hung up, we could hear her saying something to Mr. Clausen, and soon two pairs of grown-up feet were climbing the stairs.

Edgar had left the door open. I looked at them, not wanting them to speak, but Edgar didn't hesitate. "Mama's gone to that good place, hasn't she?" he asked.

Mr. Clausen arms encircled him. "Yes, she has." His voice was soft.

I had thought I was through with crying. I had known it was going to happen, hadn't I? Why was I crying? Mama was in a good place. We had a good home. Why wouldn't the tears stop?

"Oh, Rosie—we're so sorry." Mrs. Clausen wrapped me in her arms.

They stayed with us for several minutes, holding us, assuring us they'd do everything they could to help us through this.

I stopped crying finally. "We've got to call Albert and George."

"It was Mr. Sloven on the phone. The hospital called him, and he's told your brothers. They'll be coming in soon."

The Clausens and the Slovens made all the arrangements, a word I understood much better now. Mama's body was shipped to McFarland on the train, and once again, Greener's Mortuary got busy.

All four of us sat down with the Clausens and Slovens and Reverend Ritter. Since the Clausens were Methodists, and the Sloven's were Lutheran, and Reverend Ritter was Baptist, we had to decide where to hold the funeral service and what kind of service it would be.

George said, "Mama was a quiet person and I think she'd like a quiet service with probably just our family and the people who know us."

"She'd like songs, though. Mama loved to sing."

"Maybe each of you could choose one," Reverend Ritter suggested.

"Jesus Loves Me," said Edgar.

"Nearer My God to Thee," Albert decided quickly.

George chose "The Old Rugged Cross" and I picked the hymn I'd learned after Dad's funeral, "What a Friend We Have in Jesus."

Reverend Ritter had saved the information from Dad's funeral, and some information had come from the hospital, too. Our mama was 37 years old, born in 1915, nine years younger than our dad. She had grown up on a farm in Wisconsin, gone to high school and then worked in a dime store, until she married our dad when she was 22. She loved to sing and to work in the garden and bake bread. "She was real pretty,' Albert said.

"And real nice." George sounded hoarse.

"She loved us all, and she---" Albert's voice broke.

I told them about how she always wrote to her mother in Wisconsin the minute a letter came, and how she would put Edgar in the wagon, and walk to the post office down the road to mail it. "I wrote to her in the hospital, but she couldn't ever write back and—" I was a mess of sobs.

The funeral was set for January 8th, and since Reverend Ritter would be the minister, it would be at the Baptist church. It would be held at four o'clock, in case any of our school friends wished to attend.

Mrs. Clausen picked up my assignments, and I filled the time doing schoolwork, candling eggs, stocking shelves, and any cooking or housework that Mrs. Clausen needed done. I had quit crying, but inside was one huge ache.

Edgar followed Mr. Clausen around the store, went with him on errands, and drew and colored picture after picture of flowers. I couldn't imagine what he was going to do with them, but he kept working. "I'm making them for Mama," he told me, "and Miz Clausen is going to take them down to Greeners for her."

CHAPTER 15

Annie

I was furious with God, and I let Him know it. I wasn't a big pray-er, at least not like my dad. I said The Lord's Prayer every night and I never ate a bite of food without mentally reciting "God is great. God is good. Now I thank him for my food." It was only in stressful times I really talked to Him. After a New Year's Day of total sadness, broken by not even Edgar's cute speeches or a word or two with Rosie, or for that matter, Bobby popping in, I was beside myself. Rosie had stayed in her room, except for going into the bathroom, and when I called out to her, "I'm sorry, Rosie," she had only squeaked out something that sounded a little like "Thank you." Edgar went in and out of her room, but then followed my dad down to the basement where some reorganization of shelves seemed to be going on.

Bobby was helping his grandparents; the Olsens had gone to visit their grandmother in Woolsey. I tried to read my library book, but I couldn't get into it. Suddenly I found myself kneeling at the side of my bed, sobbing with anger. "Why did You do this? Can't You let people be happy for a little while? Rosie and Edgar and George and Albert were all doing just fine or almost fine. Hadn't You hurt them enough? You took their dad away, and now You've taken their mother. You didn't have to do this. You could have kept this from happening. Why didn't you? Amen."

We spent a gloomy weekend, broken only by our jobs at the store and church on Sunday, where an announcement was made about the funeral.

Bobby didn't come around asking us to go skating. My mother gave me the job of peeling potatoes and carrots for the stew we were having for supper, while she baked a cake. "Now, Annie, tomorrow you'll go back to school as usual, and after the funeral, so will Rosie. It's on Thursday right after school, so you'll need to wear a nice skirt and sweater set to school, and go right over to the Bap—"

"I'm not going. I didn't even know their mother, and I'm not—"

It was my father's voice that stopped me. "You're going, Annie. Rosie and Edgar are part of our family, and families support each other."

I nodded at both of them, tears hot on my eyes, and ran from the room.

I had been to exactly two funerals—that of my mother's older sister when I was nine, and we'd traveled to Minneapolis for it, and to Mr. Merritt's mother's funeral only last year. The thought of death was something I tried to avoid, and going to a funeral forced me to think about it.

At least going back to school got me away from Rosie's sadness, and I was glad when Bobby stopped by on Monday morning to see if I was ready for school.

"Ready for Walzak again?" He made a face.

"Guess so. My homework's done at least."

"How're Rosie and Edgar?"

"Quiet—even Edgar. Rosie just doesn't say anything. And I don't think she'll ever smile again."

"I'm going to the funeral. Least I can do for them." He sounded so grown up and sure of himself.

"Really?"

"Well, aren't you?"

"Yes. My dad said I have to, but I don't believe it will do any good. I didn't know their mother, and I doubt if they care whether or not I go."

"That's not the point. The Stample kids are our friends. You don't leave your friends hanging out to dry."

"I don't need a sermon, Reverend Merritt," I said as I ran up the steps of the school.

That was the way the whole week went. We'd start a conversation off friendly enough, and in no time, I'd find myself ready to argue with him.

At home, Rosie and Edgar were very quiet, and I couldn't think what to say to them. I wanted them to know how sorry I was, how sad I was, but if I said anything, I thought it might make them feel worse.

Dressed in my new navy blue skirt and sweater, white knee socks and saddle shoes. I wearily made my way back to school after lunch on Thursday, hands stuffed in the pockets of my gray wool dress coat.

I heard him behind me and stopped for a moment, waiting for him to catch up. He, too, was dressed up—black trousers and gray winter coat. I broke a strict rule I had with myself to never compliment Bobby. "You look nice," I found myself saying.

"Thanks. You do, too."

"Thanks. I wish we were dressed up for something fun."

"I bet Rosie and Edgar do, too."

"I just meant—oh, never mind!" Would I never be able to have a conversation with Bobby again, without him making me feel guilty for what I'd said?

I was amazed at how many usually blue-jeaned boys wore dress slacks that day—Billy Olsen, Zack Jones, Bobby, and several others who were becoming friendly with Albert and George. They were all a bit more serious that afternoon.

We were always called to Study Hall for final announcements. That day Mr. Stillwater announced that those attending the Stample funeral should get their coats and books and things and leave the building first.

I followed Evelyn and Elizabeth, and Bobby followed their brother. If anyone knew the workings of the Baptist church and funeral decorum, it was the Olsens. We found Mrs. Olsen just inside the church door, and she whispered for all of us to follow her. Two of the frontmost pews had been reserved for students. I had planned to sit with my parents, but then I saw they were across the aisle and in the very front. I sat between Evelyn and Bobby and concentrated hard on the altar.

The church was quite full. The people of McFarland had developed a very soft spot for the Stample kids in a very short time.

I might have been fine, had I stared straight ahead, but when the casket was carried up the aisle by six Baptist men, and I saw Rosie and Edgar walking so solemnly behind it, I felt the tears start. Jamming my hands in my pockets, I was horrified to discover I had no handkerchief! Wasn't that the last thing my mother had reminded me of? I put my hands to my eyes and tried very hard to not think of the hurt in Rosie's heart. My eyes seemed to be producing a rainstorm. I tried my skirt pocket again. It was then I felt a handkerchief in my hand—Bobby's handkerchief. "Thank you," I mouthed.

I suppose, if you go to enough funerals to judge them fairly, Mrs. Stample's funeral was way above average. The hymns were lovely, and the Reverend Ritter announced which child had chosen each hymn. We all joined in on "Jesus Loves Me." It was a funeral where one felt hard pressed to keep from crying. It was as if the sadness index made Mrs. Stample's funeral above average.

Mrs. Stample's story helped me to understand a lot of things and made me worry, too. She had been a happy woman, loving her family, taking care of them, singing. And then one day all her happiness collapsed around her. And then, the Reverend Ritter, though, found hope. "When we had Mr. Stample's funeral here last fall, we were a town of strangers to the Stamples. In the months since, however, we've come to know and love and respect this family. Let us hold them in our hearts and pray for them daily."

Since it was so cold and so much snow covered the cemetery, the burial would happen later, and Greeners would let the Clausens and Slovens know when to come to the cemetery for it.

A potluck dinner awaited everyone downstairs. I took my cues from Elizabeth Olsen who walked over to Rosie and Edgar and offered them her sympathy. Bobby followed Elizabeth. "I'm so sorry," he told Rosie, and he hugged Edgar.

"It's okay, Bobby. Mama is in that good place—just like Dad. And Jesus is there, with them."

I was stunned at Edgar's speech because he'd been so quiet at home. Without missing a beat, Bobby said. "You're right, Edgar."

George and Albert thanked us for coming. We filled our plates and joined the Stamples. We were soon followed by Zack Jones and all the Olsens. I tried to think of something to say, but as always, Bobby jumped right in first. "You guys gonna all want to skate on Sunday afternoon?"

I wasn't sure it was even a proper question to ask those who were grieving. I was sure Rosie would demur, but I heard her quiet "I do," along with everyone elses. The Slovens were spending Sunday afternoon in town playing Canasta, a card game that was all the rage now, so George and Albert were more than eager.

"Let's meet at the pond at 1:30," said Zack, and it was agreed upon.

I saw my mother and Mildred motioning to me. "You and Bobby need to go help at the store." They were going to help the Baptists clean. Rosie and Edgar and their big brothers were talking to the Reverend Ritter.

We crunched through the snow, hurrying as the air around us grew colder.

I pulled my coat tight around myself. "Thanks for lending me your hankie," I said. "You saved me from a ton of embarrassment."

He grinned. "Good thing I had two. You got it pretty soggy." It wasn't the most gracious thing he could have said, but it didn't matter. We were friends again, and everything might have been just Jim Dandy if Mary Lou Minders hadn't moved to town.

CHAPTER 16

Rosie

The dull ache didn't go away. My brothers seemed to be healing, and Edgar became his old self quite quickly.

I had thought school might help, but I only went through the motions. Miss Graud had divided our class into two math groups, and it was easy to tell she had placed me in the group covering the more difficult material. Sometimes for a few seconds when I concentrated on a problem, I would forget the pain. But it always came back.

I helped at the store, preferring to stay away from customers, but working extra hard at whatever I was asked to do. Annie invited me to play Monopoly and I did, but behind every action, was a gray, painful longing. It wasn't exactly for my mother, but for a connection to her. I couldn't write to her now. At night I cried myself to sleep, head buried in my pillow.

On Sunday, though, I couldn't wait to get to the pond, and for the two hours we were there, gliding across the ice, I could feel Mama and Dad. It was like they each held one of my hands. Sometimes I skated with the other girls or in a big circle, but mostly I flew up and down the pond alone. I wasn't aware there was a smile on my face, but Edgar came up and said, "I'm glad you're happy, Rosie."

It wasn't until we were ready to walk home that I saw the new girl. Even in the fog I was in, I noticed her. Elizabeth introduced her. "This is Mary Lou Minders. They just moved into the old Crawford house."

She was beautiful. We all saw that at once. Dark black hair in a stylish poodle cut, though most of her hair was covered with a bright red stocking cap, green eyes with dark lashes, and a smile of perfect teeth. She was in seventh grade and had lots of questions for Annie and Elizabeth and Evelyn about classes.

When it was time to go, I was the last one off the ice, and walking home, the grayness came back.

Monday night, I finished my homework and headed upstairs to bed. Mrs. Clausen knocked on my door and came in with a box for me. "These are for you, Rosie. The letters you wrote to your mother. All in this box."

"Thank you."

She stopped and folded me in her arms." It will get better, Rosie. I promise."

Mrs. Clausen would know, I thought. She'd been orphaned when she was young. I put the letters on the top shelf of the closet, and tried not to cry. I stared at the ceiling.

I knew there was one thing that would make me feel better, but I had to wait until everyone was asleep. I put on my long underwear and jeans and two sweaters and crawled back under the covers. One thing about the Clausens was everyone went to bed by 9:30. They worked hard all day, and they were exhausted.

At ten, I tiptoed down the stairs and went out the back door, skates across my shoulders. The North Dakota winter air was cold, but once I was on the ice, I was warm. I could feel Mama and Dad holding my hands and skating with me. Over and over I flew across the pond.

I stayed until I heard voices from a yard across the creek—someone calling their dogs to come in. I ran part of the way home. I was cold and tired when I finally lay back down to sleep. The little clock on my bedstand said 11:30, and I fell asleep quickly.

Next morning I awoke to Annie's voice. "Better hurry up. Mom came up quite awhile ago." I dressed hurriedly, and slogged through the day. For a little while, though, I'd escaped the pain.

I would go back to the pond many nights, and for quite a long time, I got away with it.

CHAPTER 17

Annie

School settled down to a grind now that the holidays were over. Apparently the faculty had met and decided we all needed more homework, so in our household, there wasn't much time for fun except on weekends. McFarland High School had a good basketball team, and a big share of the townsfolk devoted Friday nights to attending basketball games. My parents, of course, couldn't go, and I was only permitted to attend home games. However, there were three home games in a row in January, and I got caught up in the excitement. I tried to talk Rosie into accompanying me, and I assumed, Bobby, but she said she just didn't feel like going.

It seemed as if Rosie would be sad forever. The only time she appeared to be happy was skating on the pond, and then she seemed to be off in another world. I think we were all worried about her, but no one could say she didn't do what was expected of her—and sometimes way more.

On the Thursday night before we played Woolsey, I decided to lay out my outfit for the next day—a green, long-sleeved cotton shirt and black skirt. "Mom, my shirt's in the laundry, and I need it for tomorrow for the pep assembly." I called down the stairs.

My mother didn't answer, so I ran down with the shirt. "Annie, you know the rules around here. Laundry gets done on Monday, and whatever isn't in it has to wait for next week. Wear something else."

"But we're all wearing these shirts for the assembly."

My mother did not see the point at all. Other mothers did their own ironing, but my mother never had. Mildred Merritt did our laundry, and my mother did her baking, and they were both quite happy about it; but it was certainly causing me an inconvenience. I stormed back upstairs, and knocked on Rosie's door. "Guess what? I don't have a shirt for the assembly tomorrow."

Rosie looked like she'd been crying again, but she sat up and after a moment said, "Why can't you wear that one?"

"It's dirty."

"Can't you just wash it out by hand?"

"Maybe, but it would have to be ironed."

She probably wanted to say, "Well, then iron it." But, instead she seemed to realize I had never ironed anything in my whole life. "I'll iron it for you," she said.

She followed me down to the basement, where there were laundry supplies. It is not quite accurate to say my mother didn't do laundry. She washed clothes, but sent what needed ironing to Mildred. I ran some water and hesitated a little. Rosie added some soap flakes and swished her hands back and forth in the water, waiting for the soap to dissolve. She took the shirt and sloshed it up and down and rubbed a tiny spot on the sleeve out. I ran more water, and we rinsed it out. She wrung the water out of it, and we hung it on the clothesline that was strung across the basement. The furnace was down there, and the shirt would dry quickly.

An hour later it was just a little damp. "It's perfect for ironing. Where's the iron?"

"I don't know if we have one." We began checking the cupboards, but both of us came up empty.

"You know Mildred Merritt does our ironing, don't you?" She hadn't known that. I looked out the window.

The lights were still on at the Merritts. "Come on. Shh—we'll have to slip out the back door." We didn't put on our coats or anything, just hurried across the yard to the Merritt's back door. Thankfully, Bobby opened it, and we explained our need for an iron. "Come on downstairs. Grandma's got it all set up. But they're asleep, so quiet!"

Rosie worked quickly, and the blouse was ironed in ten minutes' time. "Good job, Rosie," Bobby said.

"Thanks, I appreciate it." I told her when we got home. "I guess I'd better learn to press my own stuff. too."

"I can teach you. I had to learn when my mother got sick."

"Annie and Rosie, time for bed. School tomorrow," my mother called up the stairs.

Walking to school next morning, Bobby told us he would be going to the game with Zack Jones, that he'd see us there. It seemed a little odd, but Bobby and Zack often did things together. Rosie had slipped back into herself and didn't say a word.

CHAPTER 18

Rosie

I knew I shouldn't be sneaking out to go skating without permission, but whatever guilt I may have had was more than compensated for by the peace I felt as I skated. It was as if I could feel Mama and Dad holding my hands and skating with me. We seemed to fly over the ice, and as we flew comfort filled my being. I was careful to only go on "school" nights—those being Monday through Thursday – and only after ten p.m. So far I'd been lucky. I'd never met another person, though once I'd sworn I'd heard a stifled cough.

There was a problem, though. Besides the twinges of guilt, I was having a hard time getting up in the mornings. Annie had been really good about warning me, if I wasn't up in time for Mrs. Clausen's quick inspections on school days, and also, to be sure I ate breakfast—a definite requirement in the Clausen household.

The morning of the pep rally I was especially tired and only drug myself out of bed. I had a green school sweater, which I put on with a gray skirt. I had trouble with my pony tail, which Mrs. Clausen quickly fixed, but not before she noticed my droopiness. "Rosie, aren't you sleeping well? You seem awfully tired."

"I'm okay." She seemed unconvinced. For a moment, I considered telling her about my nighttime forays to the skating pond, but my courage failed me.

School was difficult that day. I even lagged in math, and Miss Graud seemed surprised when I struggled. Fortunately she explained multiplying one fraction by another again, and the second time I caught on. At recess she stopped me and asked how I felt. "You seem awfully tired today, Rosie. Are you feeling unwell?"

"No, I'm fine." Another lie. Would I ever be fine again?

At 3:00 the elementary students began to be dismissed to walk to the high school gym for the pep rally. We were seated in the bleachers behind the junior high school students. Annie turned and waved at me. She sat beside Ellen Lassen, another seventh grader, and well away from the little group closer to the floor. Bobby, the Olsen twins, and Zack Jones were totally absorbed in whatever Mary Lou Minders was saying. A chorus of laughter erupted, and then Bobby must have said something hilarious because suddenly all eyes were on him.

I looked at Annie who was talking earnestly to Ellen, and almost decided that Annie didn't care that she wasn't in the group, but then I saw her eyes drift away from Ellen's for just a second to look at Mary Lou's crowd, and I knew Annie wasn't happy. I didn't have much sympathy for her. She had her parents, both of them, I thought.

The Boy Scout troop marched in carrying the flag, and we all saluted it. The band played the National Anthem, and we remained standing, hands crossed over our hearts. Then the high school basketball players walked in and were seated across the gym from us, in the center of the first row. We yelled and cheered as the coach announced their names and positions. Next the four cheerleaders, the prettiest girls in the whole school, Jennifer Olsen had told me, walked to the center of the gym and the performance began. Even I knew the yells by now, and I yelled along with everyone else. Inside I was wondering how I'd get through tonight without going skating, without being with Mama and Dad.

CHAPTER 19

Annie

To say that Mary Lou Minders was anything but beautiful would have been to just out and out lie. She became a part of our 7th grade class right after the semester began, and every student, boy and girl alike, was keen to help her catch up, to become friends with her, No one was more eager to help, of course, than Bobby, unless it might have been Zack Jones. The Olsen girls quickly showed her the ropes like the quickest way to get from class to class, and also warned her about Mr. Walzak. That gentleman seemed to ignore her, and Mary Lou evidently was doing well enough in math that he had not decided to make a spectacle of her—yet. It took me a good week to realize Bobby and Zack were seeing that Mary Lou's math was done correctly. Bobby was always hurrying off to find Zack if we got to school early.

Mary Lou also needed help with English, and Elizabeth and I had offered to help her during the free period after lunch on Monday, Wednesday, and Friday, but somehow she never was able to make it—said she had to get math help. On the day of the pep assembly, Miss Javitz, the English instructor, gave a pop quiz. It was simple enough, underlining a specific part of speech in each sentence. Not worried about embarrassing anyone, Miss Javitz had us correct each other's papers as she read answers. She then had the papers passed back and called out our names, so we could each shout out our percentage of correct answers. It saved her time correcting papers, and she was not the slightest bit concerned over anyone not being able to do the math—Mr. Walzak had surely seen to that—nor about embarrassing anyone. Mary Lou's score was 45%, and the next lowest was an 80%.

Miss Javitz knitted her eyebrows together. "Miss Minders, did you not get some help from Miss Clausen and Miss Olsen?"

Mary Lou's face was ashen. "No."

"Why not?"

"They were too busy when I had time."

"When did you have time?"

"Just in the mornings."

I inhaled sharply. Mary Lou Minders had told a bold faced lie. I raised my hand, but Miss Javitz ignored me. She also ignored Elizabeth. "You will take the quiz over tomorrow morning, Miss Minders. I suggest you find someone who has time to tutor you."

Bobby and Zack both got out their English books and carried them to the pep rally. Elizabeth shrugged the whole thing off. "I don't think Mary Lou understood us," she said.

"I don't understand her," I said. "I'm going to sit with Ellen. See you later." Ellen was our pastor's daughter. She was very quiet and well-behaved, and I liked her fine. I wanted, though, to be with Bobby and the Olsens and even with Zack, but I didn't want to ever see Mary Lou Minders again. I tried to think of things to talk to Ellen about: our Sunday school class, had she memorized the bible verses, and was she going to the skating party on Sunday afternoon. She asked if I thought Rosie was getting better, and I said I didn't know. Once we started cheering, I yelled as loud as anybody. I waited for Rosie to walk home together. She was quiet as always, and the fact she didn't ask rude questions was one of the things I liked best about Rosie.

Mom took one look at us and poured milk and set out oatmeal cookies. Then she said, "Rosie, you go get a nap. You look awfully tired. Edgar and Annie can both do a little extra tonight."

Usually Rosie would have protested, but today relief swept across her face. Edgar asked, "Is Bobby going to help us?"

"No, he told Mildred he and Zack have something important to do at school, so the Merritts are both staying late, too."

I set my lips and intended on not talking to anyone at all, just working like crazy, but I hadn't counted on Edgar's cheerful banter. "Come on,

Annie. I'll race you to fill the bottom shelves. I want to do the peas and carrots. You do the green beans."

"You're on," I said. We finished shelving and began flattening cardboard boxes. There were eggs to be candled, and as we worked, Edgar asked me riddles. He and the young Olsens had been exchanging them. "What's black and white and red all over, Annie?"

"A newspaper."

"Right, now you ask me one."

"I can't think of any." The biggest riddle of my life was what was Bobby Merritt thinking.

I didn't want to go to the game, but I called Elizabeth to see if she was going. She wasn't feeling like it, she said, but Evelyn wanted someone to go with her. I told her I'd meet Evelyn at 6:45, and I also called Ellen to see if she wanted to sit with us. So it was agreed upon, and I spent the whole evening wondering what Bobby, Zack, and Mary Lou were talking about. McFarland beat Woolsey 58 -57 in an overtime game, and I didn't have any fun at all.

The next day Miss Javitz announced that Mary Lou Minders had happily received a passing mark on her second attempt, and that she, Miss Javitz, was grateful to whoever had stepped up and helped out a fellow student.

CHAPTER 20

Rosie

I awoke in a dark room and wondered what day it was. I wasn't tired any longer, and I could just feel the edges of sadness breaking through my consciousness. I looked at the little alarm clock and was surprised it was 9:00. Finally I remembered Mrs. Clausen telling me to take a nap. I had slept a solid five hours. Everyone would be in bed soon, and they must be wondering about me. And Edgar hadn't even come around to say good night.

Downstairs I found Mrs. Clausen mending a shirt and Mr. Clausen reading. "My goodness, Rosie, you were one tired girl." She hurried to the fridge. "We had chicken noodle soup for supper. I'll just heat you up a bowl."

It tasted awfully good, and so did the piece of apple pie she cut for me. The Clausens were so kind to us, and I felt quite bad about sneaking out to go skating, but it was the only way the sadness would lift. I told myself I'd quit going soon, but every chance I got, I went.

I washed up my dishes and wiped off the place I'd eaten from. "Any homework, Rosie? Better get started on it."

Thankfully, I'd gotten it all done in study hall, except for my English. I knew Mrs. Clausen would check it, and she did. "Rosie, what's the rule for come or came?" I read it to her right out of the grammar book, and then proceeded to correct three out of twenty sentences I had wrong. She gave me a hug, and said, "You might as well wait up for Annie with us. She should be here any minute. I think the girls were going to get a coke after the game."

"Did Edgar---?" I started to ask if he'd wanted to say good night to me, but that seemed silly.

"He wanted to wake you, but we thought you really needed your rest." Mr. Clausen patted my shoulder, and then said, "Here's Annie now."

She came in quietly and announced, "We beat Woolsey 58 to 57 in an overtime."

"Well, you don't seem real happy about it," her dad observed.

"Guess I don't really care," Annie answered. She cut herself a piece of pie and told her dad that Philip Jones, Zack's older brother, had made the layup that put us over the top.

"We'd better get to bed," Mrs. Clausen said. "I think we're all just tired."

Upstairs, I said good night to Annie, brushed my teeth, and washed my face and hands and crawled into bed. I wasn't tired now, and nobody would be on the pond. I got back out of bed and slipped into jeans and two sweaters and waited. Softly, I descended the stairs and crept out the back door.

Once I was on ice, I could feel Mom and Dad holding my hands, but somehow I felt like they were telling me I mustn't come any more, that I had to let go of them and live my life. "No," I whispered, "I need you! Let me keep coming. Please!"

It was as if the hands let go, and I dropped mine. I tried raising my hands again, but I couldn't feel them. Suddenly I heard someone on the path, but I couldn't see anyone. I changed back into my boots and ran to the Clausens in record time. I lay in bed staring at the ceiling, feeling terribly alone. Going back to the pond wouldn't be easy now. Did I even want to? And who had been on the path? Was I in danger or had I imagined the whole thing? And why were Mama and Dad telling me not to come back?

Chapter 21

Annie

I drug myself out of bed and took a shower, and then woke Rosie, who seemed sadder than ever. It was Saturday, and there was lots to do as my mother had said. She waited for us at the kitchen table, along with an exuberant Edgar, who was thrilled to be going to Bismarck with Dad to take a look at the latest farm machinery and some hardy seeds. Mom, Rosie, and I were to run the store today with help from the Merritts, if needed. I knew Mom wanted the Merritts to have a weekend off and would only bother them in a total emergency. There was one member of the Merritt family I was never going to bother with again.

We'd just finished our cereal and toast, when Dad appeared and said, "Ready to go, Edgar?"

"Yessiree!" shouted Edgar. He stopped and gave Rosie a hug. "Don't be so sad, Rosie," he told her softly.

"Bye, Annie. Bye, Miz Clausen."

The store took everybody's effort. Mom assigned Rosie to cleaning shelves in the back and me to stocking bread and candy. Then I cleaned shelves in the front, and Rosie stocked what produce had come in. It was winter, and our produce tended to be scanty, but today oranges, apples, and bananas had arrived. I worked as quickly as I could. Suddenly the bell that signaled a gas customer rang, and I hurried out front. I kept an old jacket and gloves in the back of the store now.

I filled the gas tank of Mr. Lewis, the town's one and only lawyer, and quickly made change for him. He was about to drive away when I realized Bobby was standing behind me. "Nicely done, Miz Clausen!"

I ignored him. Another customer needed gas and I gave her, Miss Javitz, my full attention. She, though, was looking at Bobby. "I so appreciate all the help you and Zack are giving Mary Lou. She was so pleased you two went to her house and helped her. It's just so gentlemanly of you both."

"Two dollars and eighty nine cents," I said in a most businesslike tone, I hoped. She counted out the exact change. "Thank you. Have a nice weekend."

She drove off, and Bobby said, "I need to talk to you. It's important."

"I'm too busy to talk to you at the moment, Mr. Merritt."

"Fine. I'll just have to take matters into my own hands. I really could have used your help." He turned and walked away.

January blurred into February, and I got into basketball games. Evelyn and Ellen and I went together. McFarland was having a really good year and school spirit was high. Elizabeth liked the pep rallies, but rarely attended the games.

As for Bobby, I didn't speak to him except in the presence of our parents. He and Zack must have spent hours helping Mary Lou as she seemed to be doing much better. And then one day, Walzak was in a very bad mood. He'd begun to introduce algebra to the class, and most of us had sense enough to be terrified we'd be called to the board. Mary Lou smiled sweetly and pretended to be concentrating, all the while writing a note on a small scrap of paper. She sat on one side of me, and I could see she was shifting to the right slightly. Walzak turned his back to demonstrate finding the value of x, and Mary Lou passed the note to Bobby. Apparently, some people really do have eyes in the back of their heads, I thought, as Walzack spun around and pounced on Bobby.

"Read the note, Mr. Merritt."

"I can't. Please—No!"

Walzak grabbed the note and gleefully read, *"Dear Bobby, Please come by the house after school. I need help again. I can't understand this old goat at all. MLM."*

"Well, Mr. Merritt, or shall we say, Dear Bobby, another fair damsel has fallen under your spell! Isn't that interesting? Miss Clausen, what do you think of this?" He stood above me and clearly expected me to answer. I hesitated, hoping he'd go away.

"Well?"

"I think nothing of it at all," I lied. "It is not my concern." I stared straight ahead and felt white-hot indignation rise within me. Why should I be publicly humiliated because Mary Lou Minders was stupid enough to write a note to Bobby in his class. And why was he not picking on her? Why me? No matter how many times I might have thought it, I would never have been so brazen to write the words "Old goat" in his class. Or so dumb, I thought.

"Well, Mr. Merritt, this old goat does hope you'll be able to get Miss MLM sorted out as far as her equations go. This old goat will appreciate it." He turned back to his lecture. We stared straight ahead, except for Elizabeth, who had managed a sideways glance. Mary Lou's face was pink, she told us, as we walked home, but Bobby's was white.

"Poor Bobby! He can't catch a fair shot with Walzak. And why would Mary Lou do such a foolish thing?"

"I could care less," I told her. "Let's get a coke. No orders tonight, and Rosie and Edgar are taking a turn."

The soda fountain counter was packed today. Notably absent were Zack Jones, Mary Lou Minders, and Bobby. Suddenly the idea of standing in line for a coke didn't appeal to me at all. Elizabeth had gone off with Ellen to check out the new records.

The Union was busy, and even though I was supposed to be off, I joined Edgar and Rosie straightening up the produce section. I wouldn't have noticed the older couple usually, because I concentrated on my work and didn't pay attention to the customers unless they asked for something. It was this couple's conversation that caught my attention.

"I want to get some more of those red potatoes and a nice roast," said the woman. "Those boys seem to like that, and I like seeing Mary Lou so happy. And long as they help her, she can get decent grades."

"Okay," the man said, "but we gotta watch our pennies. The rent's coming due."

"Already?" asked the woman.

"Yes, and he's not gonna be patient this time. I think those boys could eat soup just like we do."

"Oh, now Harold, let's not worry about it tonight. Get a package of cookies and a carton of ice cream." The man sighed and did as his wife said.

I suddenly understood way more than I wanted to, and I wished I'd never heard of Mary Lou Minders.

CHAPTER 22

Rosie

February was basketball games and cold weather. McFarland was having a good season with 15 wins and only 2 losses, and the town had great hopes of going to the state tournament the first weekend in March. I didn't care that much about basketball, but there seemed no way to get out of going to home games. If Annie and Evelyn didn't insist on my going, my own brothers would come by to take Edgar and me. Albert and George were both thinking of going out for the team next year and they studied the game intently. We'd sit high in the bleachers, and they'd quietly explain the game to Edgar and me.

The third week of February, the district tournament was held in McFarland, and on Saturday, McFarland beat Woolsey 72—67. The yelling and cheering was unbelievable, and the whole student body, it seemed, headed to the drugstore to celebrate. Bobby and Zack Jones were holding down a booth, and they waved for us to come over. Edgar, of course, was thrilled to scoot in beside Bobby, and we followed him. Since Annie wasn't speaking to Bobby these days, I was uncomfortable, but when she came bouncing in with Evelyn and Ellen moments later, Edgar, couldn't contain himself. "Hey, Annie! We're over here."

Annie turned and smiled at Edgar and our older brothers. "Hi Guys." She then walked away with her friends.

"Why doesn't Annie sit with us?" Edgar looked square at Bobby.

"I don't know."

I tried to shush Edgar. "You'll see her at home. Now what would you li—" Edgar was not finished.

"Well, where is that other girl? You know—the pretty one."

Bobby looked stunned. "I don't know anything about any girls."

This time George spoke sternly to Edgar. "Stop asking questions that aren't any of your business. It's not polite."

And that might have been it, if Mary Lou hadn't appeared on the scene. She wore a bright red hat and coat, and was alone. She appeared not to see anyone and headed into the back of the store where aspirin and other over-the-counter remedies were sold. Edgar couldn't contain himself. "She's there, Bobby, back there buying something."

"Edgar, we're going home—right now!" I said.

"Just a minute, Rosie. I'll walk with you guys," Bobby said. I was way more stunned than anyone. Surely Bobby would want to stay at the drugstore where all his friends celebrating.

We told our brothers goodbye and began the short walk home. Edgar chattered away with Bobby about everything that went on at the store, and how he was going to play basketball when he grew up. He hurried into the house when we got home, yelling "Bye, Bobby." I hoped that neither the Merritts nor the Clausens were sleeping.

"Thanks for walking back with us, Bobby."

"Rosie, wait. I need to talk to you."

I stopped with my hand just ready to turn the knob. "What about?"

"I know you've been going to the skating pond alone. You've got to stop it. If anyone finds out, you'll be in trouble."

So Bobby was the one I'd heard. "Please don't tell on me. Please."

"Nobody's ever supposed to go there alone—and soon the ice—"

I didn't let him finish. "Okay. Only please don't tell. Please."

He only said, "See you later, Rosie." I thought he'd go back to the drugstore, but he went across the yard to his own house.

The Clausens were still up. I told them Annie was with Evelyn and that Bobby and I had walked Edgar home early. They'd heard about Mc Farland winning the game, of course.

"Rosie, Mrs. Jim called. She wanted to know if you and Edgar could come Saturday night next week instead of Thursday—her relatives from

Williston will be here. I told her I'd have you call her first thing in the morning."

"All right. It's fine with me."

Dear Mrs. Jim. Always trying to cheer me up. I didn't know if I'd ever be cheered up again. Not really. In bed I lay thinking about the ice, wanting to go skating, and knowing I couldn't. I hoped Bobby wouldn't tell on me.

CHAPTER 23

Annie

McFarland was all abuzz. We would play Herring for the regional title and the chance to go to the state tournament in Fargo in two weeks. The regional game would be in Bismarck this coming Friday, and Evelyn and Ellen and I were determined to go. We decided that our best chance of accomplishing that feat was for each of us to ask our fathers to drive us. Surely one of them would agree. In a perfect world, Bobby and Rosie and Edgar and I would ride with my father or Bobby's grandfather, but it was no longer a perfect, or even a good world. And I would just have to get use to the fact that Bobby Merritt was no longer my best friend. He wasn't really my friend, period.

I brought up the subject at breakfast. "Isn't it wonderful good old McFarland is finally going to the regionals at last? Guess what, Dad. Zack Jones' dad saw Herring play last week when he went up there, and he's sure McFarland can beat them!"

"My goodness, haven't you become enthusiastic, Annie!"

"Well aren't you?"

"I'm glad we won, but---"

"You'll take us, won't you, Dad? I'd feel very embarrassed not going the one and only time McFarland gets a chance to play."

My parents both stared at me. Finally, my father said, "I will consider it, Annie, and that is all I can say for now."

He was such a good dad. I smiled at him.

"You want to go, don't you Rosie?"

She hesitated a second and seemed to think of something. "No that's the night Mrs. Jim wants Edgar and me next week."

"I'm sure she'd change it, Rosie."

"I'd really rather go to Mrs. Jim's, but thank you for asking me."

I was up early the next day, making sure I caught Dad at breakfast. He was reading the paper and drinking coffee and it seemed as if he was enjoying being alone and quiet. My mother hadn't appeared yet. And Edgar and Rosie wouldn't be up for a few more minutes.

I put bread in the toaster and fixed my bowl of corn flakes. I poured a glass of orange juice and began carrying things to the table. "Morning, Dad."

"Good morning, Annie."

"Have you thought about---"

"No, and Annie, I really want to read this paper." Well, that was that, but I'd ask again at noon.

We met in front of the school doors. Evelyn reported that Mr. Olsen was scheduled to work late at the post office that evening, and Ellen's father had flat said no, there was no way he could afford to drive to Bismarck and their car wasn't working all that well. I told them my father was considering it.

Evelyn thought of something, "Doesn't Mr. Merritt go sometimes?" she asked me pointedly.

"I know nothing about their plans," I said. No way was I going anywhere with Bobby Merritt.

My mother waited for Rosie and me at lunchtime. "Dad had to go to Woolsey with some feed, so Mildred's watching the store and Bobby is coming here for lunch."

"I'm not very hungry—I'll just get a glass of milk—"

"Sit down, Annie. I made macaroni and cheese, just the way you like it. And I need to talk to you."

I sat down, and I prayed. I prayed Bobby wouldn't show up. God must have thought my prayer rather petty, because Bobby appeared immediately. He was in a jolly mood.

"Oh, Mrs. Clausen. Is that your famous mac and cheese? Isn't it good, Rosie? Where's Edgar?"

"He went to Woolsey, too" my mother said, sure that Mildred had explained why she was working, why he was eating with us.

I took only a small portion and ate it quickly. "May I be excused?"

My mother looked at me intently. "No, Annie. I told you I need to talk to you. Dad and the Merritts and I checked the schedule at the store, and Dad absolutely has to be at the store on Friday. Some of the farmers' supply orders are coming in, and he's the only one who can handle those. Merle had already agreed to take Bobby and Zack, and he says you and two friends can ride in the back seat."

"I- I don't know if—"

My mother said, "Don't you think what you should really say is that you appreciate Bobby's grandfather taking you?"

"I appreciate it very much, but maybe Bobby has other people he wants to take along." I didn't look at Bobby, and he said nothing.

"I need to get back to school—I'll stop at the store after school and thank Mr. Merritt."

My mother looked totally puzzled. Bobby began to tell Rosie and Edgar his latest jokes.

I had to tell the other girls. They both thought riding to Bismarck with Mr. Merritt and Bobby and Zack would be great.

I worried all afternoon. What if Bobby had already invited Mary Lou, and there wasn't room for all of us? Well, if that happened, I'd stay home.

Walzak was in as bad a mood as I was. He lit right in. "Mr. Merritt, have you been successful at helping Miss Minders, here, with her equations?"

Bobby didn't answer. Mary Lou was terribly pale, at least the only people who dared look at her reported. Walzak didn't care. "Let's see, Miss Minders, if you can solve the equation $2X = 14 + 54$. At the board, Miss Minders. This old goat is really interested."

Mary Lou approached the board, but the hand that grasped the chalk was shaking, and even writing the equation seemed very difficult for her. He had given her a fairly easy equation, I thought, but she seemed frozen. Had it been anyone else, I would have been sympathetic, but my heart held no pity that day for Mary Lou Minders.

She slammed the chalk down and stormed back to her desk, not to sit but to collect her notebook and pencil. "I will not be back," she announced clearly. "We are moving to Williston, and we leave tomorrow."

She marched out the door, and Walzak calmly asked Elizabeth Olsen to solve for x.

Walking to the drugstore after school, Elizabeth said she'd heard the Minders hadn't been able to pay their rent.

That afternoon, when I thanked Mr. Merritt for offering to drive us to Bismarck, Bobby was nowhere to be seen.

CHAPTER 24

Rosie

Friday dawned brightly. I watched Mr. Merrit, Bobby, Zach, Evelyn, and Ellen pile into the Merritt sedan happily, and I watched Annie get in almost reluctantly, as if she was going to a scary doctor's appointment. Edgar and I got busy stocking shelves. With Mr. Clausen unloading the heavy sacks of feed and fertilizer in the storage shed behind the store, it left Mrs. Clausen and us to attend to matters in the store, and to run the gas pump. I filled in at the cash register, but I was still just learning and I wasn't very fast. Mrs. Merritt had looked out her window, and noticed how busy we were, and hurried in to help. She also had a suggestion. "Show Rosie how to run the pumps. She's good at making change, and we can get caught up in here."

"Grab the old coat and gloves Annie uses, Rosie" And so the day sped by. Mr. Walzak came by to fuel his jeep. As I gave him his change, he said. "The Clausens have a good math student in you, I see."

"Thank you," I answered. It was funny. Everybody in 6th grade talked about the terrifying Herman Walzak. He didn't scare me one bit. For just a little while as I pumped gas and made change and stocked shelves, the sadness actually completely left me.

But then as the afternoon wore to a close, one of Mr. Sloven's neighbors pulled up to the pumps. As I filled his truck, he casually asked how I was doing. "Such a shame losing both your folks like that—so close together and all."

"I'm fine." I told him, but the gray heaviness was back.

Mrs. Jim was looking very happy and more and more expectant. She had made fried chicken and mashed potatoes and gravy and green beans and some light little biscuits. She'd opened a jar of plum jam, and Edgar ate ravenously. It all tasted great to me, too, but I couldn't eat very much.

"Jim has an idea," she told us. You know next week is the state tournament. If McFarland wins tonight, he'd like to take us all, and you can each bring a friend to Fargo. Jim's folks live there, and we can all stay with them."

"Wow!" Edgar shouted. "Can I bring Bobby? And Rosie, you ask Annie. We can all be together again. Thanks, Mr. Jim!"

We played pitch; we ate ice cream. Edgar chattered happily about going to Fargo. I couldn't wait to get home.

The Clausens were still up. Edgar immediately told them about Mr. Jim's offer to take all of us to Fargo for the state tournament.

"Yes, they asked us about it, and we thought you'd enjoy it," Mrs. Clausen said. "We won't worry about you if you're with the Weisels."

"They said we can each ask a friend, and I'm taking Bobby. Rosie can ask Annie."

"Well, that's up to Rosie—but it's mighty nice of Mr. and Mrs. Jim." said Mr. Clausen.

I lay in bed, tossing and turning. Did I have time to go skating before Annie and Bobby got home? Just once more to feel Mama and Dad's hands on mine, to feel their love as I skimmed over the ice. Were the Clausens going to wait up for Annie? As soon as the house got still, I'd sneak downstairs and out the back door. I didn't want to sneak—the word bothered me; even thinking it made me feel guilty—but I just had to feel Mama and Dad holding my hands one more time.

I hadn't undressed, and I grabbed my shoes and skates and a jacket. It wasn't very cold at all, and I didn't take gloves. Only a small night light burned downstairs, and that meant the Clausens were in bed. I tiptoed down the stairs and slid out the back door. I stepped into my loafers and began running. The wind was almost warm tonight. It hinted of spring.

Getting my skates on was easy tonight, without chilled fingers. At first I skated close to the edge of the pond, but the ice felt different, sort of mushy on top. I moved closer to the center of the lake, but even there I wasn't really gliding, and I couldn't feel Mama and Dad holding my hands.

Jutting into the lake was a cluster of trees that I liked to skate around. I moved toward them. Maybe it would be smoother there. I was almost touching their low branches when I heard the cracking sound. A moment later I felt the stabbing pain of freezing water on my feet and legs. "Ah—Ooh," I screamed, and reached out my hands to grab a branch. The first one I managed to grasp was too slender, and it broke as I pulled down on it. I felt myself slipping farther into the water, and I fought to find something I could hold. The ice was breaking around me as my hand struck the rough bark of a tree trunk. Somehow, I found the strength to put both of my arms that ached with cold around it and hold on for dear life. I could hear voices in my head—my parents' voices—"Pull your legs up on the ice, Rosie. But keep holding on to the tree."

Somehow I obeyed their voices. I could hear the sound of dozens of cars speeding down the main street of town. Everyone was returning from the regionals. I wondered if McFarland had won, and I hoped desperately that Bobby would check on me tonight. My teeth were chattering, and my arms and legs ached. "Dear Jesus, please help me," I pleaded over and over again.

CHAPTER 25

Annie

It was nearly 11:00 as Mr. Merritt drove into McFarland. The game had been a close one—57-56—and we should have been hoarse from all the yelling we'd done. But no—on the ride home we'd sung "Good Night, Irene" and "Mockingbird Hill" and "The Tennessee Waltz", and then we'd completed "99 Bottles of Beer." Mr. Merritt simply drove and was, I realized even then, a patient man. I might never speak to Bobby again, but I would always like both his grandparents.

He dropped off Ellen and then Zack and after that, Evelyn. When he pulled into our driveway, Bobby got out with me. "Wake up Rosie, and tell her we won."

I started to protest that I'd tell her in the morning, but he said, "NO, Now," so adamantly, I agreed.

I tiptoed up the stairs, and softly knocked on Rosie's door. No answer. I opened the door and said "Rosie" in a low voice. And then, I turned on her desk light and discovered she wasn't in her bed. I fled to my room and turned on the light and pulled up my blinds. Instantly, the pebble hit my window. I pushed it open and saw Bobby standing beneath it, as I'd known I would. "She's not here!" I spoke as loudly as I dared.

"She's on the pond," he yelled. "Come on!"

I ran back down the stairs and met my father face to face. "What's going on?'

"It's Rosie. She's gone. Bobby says she's on the pond."

"Go on," he told me. "I'll be right there." He handed me a flashlight. I ran to catch up with Bobby. How did he know where she was? I didn't ask questions. I tried to keep up with Bobby.

"She promised. She promised. I should have told your parents, but she promised she wouldn't go back out."

"What are you talking about?" I gasped out.

"Rosie's been sneaking out to go skating on the pond all winter. I tried to tell you, when I found out, but you wouldn't even listen."

I could hear myself. "I don't have time to talk to you, Mr. Merritt." In the snottiest voice I could muster up, no less.

As we neared the gate to the pond, Bobby pointed to the area where the trees grew. I handed him the flashlight. A shapeless mass lay close to one of the trees.

"It's Rosie! We gotta get to her." He stepped to the edge of the pond and immediately back as his tennies filled with ice cold water. Behind us, my father's footsteps crunched through brush. He carried another flashlight and a rope.

We could hear a faint cry near the trees. We followed my father as he made his way around the edge of the pond. His usually quiet voice rang out in the warm wind that blew. "Hold on, Rosie! We're coming. Hold on! Hold on!"

Dad wore tall, thick rubber boots, and he reached a point where he could step out on the ice a few yards and sink down in and be as close to Rosie as possible. He handed Bobby the other flashlight, and told us to both shine our lights on Rosie. "Can you hear me Rosie?" he yelled out.

We could hear her faint "Yes."

"I'm going to throw you this rope, Rosie. I'll try to get it close. Let go of the tree wih one hand and grab the rope with it. Do you understand?"

Once again, the faint "Yes." Maybe my father had perfected his roping skills on the farm years ago. I don't know, but the rope fell right next to Rosie.

He gave another direction as soon as Rosie had the rope in her hand. "You've got a strong loop in that rope, Rosie. Make it bigger and put it over your head and shoulders."

I wondered she could do anything with one cold hand, but she did as he asked, fumbling only a little. Now came the hard part. "Now Rosie you've got to stretch out on the ice so you're lying flat. Pull the rope up so it's in front of you, and grab onto it. I'm going to pull you across the ice, and you may get wetter, but it won't take long." She did as she was told. "Bobby and Annie, keep those lights on Rosie."

We watched as Rosie moved across the ice and as my father reached out and picked her up. The ice had held, though the cracking sounds were just below the surface. Two very long sighs escaped us. "Annie, run ahead, and have your mom start a tub of warm water, and call the doctor. Bobby, come help me out here.'

I flew up the path and out onto the street, running at my top speed. My mother was in her jeans and an old sweater. "I was just on my way to the pond," she said. I gave her Dad's instructions and started the warm bath water, while she phoned for the doctor. I realized the Merritts were there, and Mr. Merritt went to help my father and Bobby carry Rosie.

CHAPTER 26

Rosie

By the time we were halfway home, I came to my senses enough to realize I was being carried. "I can walk now," I told Mr. Clausen.

"You're still in your skates, Rosie," Bobby told me, "And by the time you get changed we'd be home."

"Want me to take a turn, Bobby?" Mr. Clausen asked.

"No, Rosie's pretty light, and we're almost there."

If I would have had full control of my senses, I would have been embarrassed to have Bobby Merritt carrying me. As it was, I slipped back into a state of cold, half consciousness.

I remember Mrs. Merritt getting my skates and socks off and then being led to the steamy bathroom. Mrs. Clausen and Mrs. Merritt helped me out of my clothes and into the hot tub of water and drew the shower curtain around the tub. I began to tremble, and my teeth started chattering again. Finally I began to soak in the warmth of the water, and the shaking ceased. Mrs. Merritt had ironed my pajamas and my sheets to warm them, and both women helped me up the stairs and into bed, where I fell into a long, dreamless sleep.

When I awoke to an early dawn, my throat was hurting, and I felt hot. Walking to the bathroom was very difficult. I was terribly weak. I crawled back into bed and drifted off again.

The next time I awoke was when Mrs. Clausen put her hand on my forehead. "Rosie, you're running a fever. I'm going to give you aspirin."

"My throat hurts."

"The aspirin will help it, too. Dr. Mc Mann said this might happen when I called him. He'll stop by sometime today."

She crushed the aspirin into a small dish of strawberry ice cream and then gave me a cup of hot tea to drink. She made me drink all of it and then rearranged my covers, as I fell back to sleep. I slept off and on all day. The doctor could tell I was developing a bad cold and cough and prescribed a cough syrup.

Edgar came in several times, and finally carried in some books and set up a library by my bed. "I can't read to you, Edgar. I feel too sick. My eyes hurt, and my throat is sore."

"I know. I just want to be with you."

"You may catch my cold."

"Yeah. I found out what happened. Why did you do that, Rosie? You coulda drownded. And you didn't tell anybody where you were going."

"Who told you that?"

He didn't answer, and I turned my face to the wall. I didn't want Edgar to see my tears. Did it matter who told him? It was true I had done a terrible thing—at least the sneaking out part was bad—but I had done it to be close to Mama and Dad. And how could I expect anyone to understand that?

I felt Edgar's little arms go around my neck. "I couldn't stand it if you drownded, Rosie."

"I'm sorry, Edgar. I just felt like Mama and Dad were with me on the pond, like they were holding my hands. That's why I kept going. I'm so lonesome for them."

"But they're lookin' down at us all the time, Rosie, not just on the pond. All the time."

"How do you know?" I asked my little brother.

"Cause I just know."

It really didn't tell me much, but even talking to Edgar took a tiny cold piece away.

Edgar brought toys in, and he played in my room. He sat up his farm in a corner and talked to all the animals. I slept, woke for a few minutes, and went back to sleep.

Late in the afternoon Annie came in. She'd helped at the store all day. "Hi Rosie."

"Hi"

"How are you feeling?"

"Really bad."

"You're going to be okay, once the cold goes away. Mom said that's what the doctor said. And that you need to rest. Is there anything you want me to get you?"

"Just—no. I've got everything. I'm sorry, Annie, about the whole thing."

"I'm sorry, too—but I'm glad you're okay. See you later."

Mrs. Clausen carried up my supper —a bowl of chicken noodle soup and a warm lemon drink—and watched me while I ate it. I tried to tell her I was sorry, but I choked on my words and my soup.

"Get well, Rosie. Then we'll have a long talk, but get well. And don't worry. You're not in trouble."

I slept again. The next time I woke Mr. Clausen held out pills and a glass of water. "I just brought these up so I could say 'Hi,' Rosie. You get to feeling better soon."

"I'm sorry I----" but he stopped me.

"Now Rosie, we'll talk when you're feeling better. Go back to sleep." Surprisingly, I did.

CHAPTER 27

Annie

Sunday came, and my father, Edgar, and I attended church, but my parents had let us miss Sunday School. Rosie was too sick to go, and my mother felt she should stay with her. Dad sat between us in the pew, one arm around Edgar, one around me. No one asked where Rosie and Mom were. They'd all been by the Union on Saturday and heard she wasn't feeling well. But they did ask if she was getting better. Dad said, "She's still got a fever, but it's going down."

Edgar whispered to Dad. "She'll get better, won't she?"

"Oh, yes," he answered, "and right now, let's all pray for her."

For once, I did pray fervently in church. I prayed Rosie would use better sense in the future, and never do such a foolish thing again. I prayed that she would be happy with us. I prayed she'd get really well, and I prayed she'd get so she'd love us enough she'd never want to leave us. I had realized what a neat sister she was when she'd help me launder the green shirt, and when she never asked me about Bobby Merritt, like all my other friends did.

We didn't linger after church visiting like we usually did, but hurried home to find the Slovens and Albert and George. They'd come to visit Rosie, and Mrs. Sloven had brought a pot roast with potatoes and carrots and onions, which had cooled some while they were in church, but would warm up quickly. The Slovens knew what had happened and were most thankful Rosie was safe. Edgar and his older brothers hurried upstairs to see Rosie, when Mom came down and announced she was ready for company. Dad and I sat the table for eight people. "Rosie needs to just rest," Mom said. Mom heated up a jar of green beans and added a few pieces of ham to them. She pulled out a package of rolls and made coffee and poured milk. The boys came downstairs. "Why don't all of you come for supper on Thursday? I think, by that time, Rosie will be able to eat dinner with us. And then, I think we all need to have a talk, and I'll ask the Merritts, too. Bobby's been awfully upset about this." The boys went back upstairs, but Rosie was sleeping. I helped with dishes and went outside and sat on the front porch The sun was warm and spring was playing games with us. We'd have more snowstorms, but spring was definitely coming. Albert and George and Edgar came outside, and we could hear the adult voices in conversation inside. "You going to the state tournament, Annie?"

Edgar couldn't let me answer. "Yes she's going. Mr. and Mrs. Jim are taking Rosie and me, and we each getta invite a friend, so I'm taking Bobby and Rosie's takin' Annie."

"Are you sure?" George asked.

"No," I said.

"Yes." Edgar was certain. "And Mr. and Miz Clausen even said yes, too. Just ask Rosie."

"I don't know anything about it, but maybe this came up while we were at Regionals."

"They called the Slovens, too, and said we can stay with Mr. Jim's folks, if we can get a ride. I won't go, though," Albert spoke for himself, "unless Rosie is well enough."

"We need to go, Guys," Mr. Sloven yelled out the door. "Go tell Rosie 'Bye."

Edgar followed them upstairs, and I sat alone and pulled my sweater tighter. Bobby came up the sidewalk, bouncing a softball. "Wanna play catch?"

"I guess." I followed him out to the street, where the only cars that had run down it all day were ours and the Slovens.

We hadn't played catch since last summer, and it took a few tosses to get into rhythm, but then we moved farther and farther apart and kept it up for a good forty-five minutes. I heard Mom calling me, and we headed to my house.

Bobby startled me, "Why'd she do that, Annie? She coulda been killed."

"I don't know, but Mom's arranging a big family-get-together for Thursday with you guys and the Slovens, and I think we're gonna talk about it." I wanted to apologize to Bobby for not listening when he'd tried to tell me about Rosie's trips to the pond, but the time for that had passed.

"I'll come by in the morning," he said.

"See ya," I answered. My best friend was back; now if my sister would just get well.

CHAPTER 28

Rosie

Monday morning I awoke at six and not hearing Annie in the bathroom, I went in for a shower. At first the warm water felt good, but when I climbed out of the shower, I started to shake again. I toweled off quickly, brushed my teeth, and ran a brush through my wet hair, and stumbled back to my room. I found a clean pair of pajamas and got back into bed, my teeth chattering, my hands shaking. When Mrs. Clausen came in, she carried some hot tea, aspirin and two pieces of toast, but when she saw how shaky I was, she stuck the thermometer under my tongue. After she read it, she poured the hot tea in a cup and added some honey and lemon juice. "Drink this, Rosie. I'm going to phone the doctor again."

I drank a little tea and fell asleep again. I could hear Annie's voice; I could hear her mother, and finally a man's voice. He simply touched my forehead. "I'm going to give her a shot of penicillin—I think she's got something more than a cold." The shot in my rear stung and burned and even ached, but then sleep took over again.

When I awoke again, Edgar stood by my bed. "I got good news, Rosie."

"Hmmm?"

"I got a letter about kindergarten. It starts next week for kids like me and I can go—Miz Clausen said so. You gotta get well, Rosie, so we can work on words and numbers again."

It seemed so long ago Edgar and I had worked on his letters and numbers. I knew everyone was always helping him with something, but I had gotten bogged down with sadness, and it had been a very long time—months, really—since I'd helped him. "I will help you just as soon as I can, Edgar." I had to get well.

I found my bathrobe and in the bathroom brushed my hair and teeth again and ran a cool washcloth across my face. Apparently the penicillin was working. I felt better than I had since Friday. Edgar had alerted Mrs. Jim, who was helping out at the store, that I was awake, and she came upstairs with more tea and applesauce and toast. She was very pregnant and beautiful and we were so glad to see each other. She hugged me for a long time. "Oh, Rosie. I'm glad you're feeling better. Now you eat this, and I'll tell you all about everything."

If we took the trip to the state championships, that was to be her last out-of-town trip until the baby came—and that was only two months away. She'd sewn all the blankets and baby clothes, and Mr. Jim had the nursery all painted, and they'd just gotten it decorated. She had found some cute little ornaments and a lamp and some toys and pillows that she wanted me to come down and arrange. She said Jim was just sure the baby would be a boy, but she was just as sure it would be a girl. "I want your help so much, Rosie."

Finally I asked, "Did they tell you what I did?"

She nodded slowly and said, "I only know everyone wants you to be happy—everyone."

"Thank you," I said softly.

After Mrs. Jim left, I pulled the chair from behind my desk over to the closet. Up there were photos of Mom and Dad, maybe one of all of us. I remembered hiding them from Ilse and bringing them here. I pulled the box down, but not before I knocked another box onto the floor. The stack of letters I'd written Mama, and had never gotten an answer from, were tied with a blue ribbon, and they landed under the chair. I had told myself I'd never look at those letters again, but seeing them there, held tight with the bow, made me realize those letters had been collected and kept, and maybe that showed they'd meant more to Mama than I'd thought. The earliest letters—those written when we first moved to McFarland—were still on top. I was in fourth grade, and we'd gone to Bismarck, and Edgar and I had shopped in the dime store for a tablet and writing pen.

I opened the first one and smiled just a little at my handwriting and some of my spelling:

Deer Mama,

> *Dad took us to Bizmarck and Edgar and I went to Woolworths. I got a comb, a tablet a pen, and a little bag of candy.*
>
> *School is hard. When we got here, Dad stayed home one day and we got settled in. There is hot and cold running water so it is easier to do wash. I'm not good at irning, but Dad helps sometimes. Miz Rodinsky taught me to make beans and some other easy things and Dad taught me to make cornbread. He always fixes us oatmeal. I wish I could do things like you did. Please Mama, come back to us soon.*
>
> *Albert and George are always busy with stuff. Edgar goes to Mrs. Chidler's while were in school.*

> *I love you Mama.*
> *Rosie*

My eyes were moist, but I refused to cry any more. I refolded the letter and tried to push it back in the envelope, but it keep getting stuck on something. I dug into the envelope then, and pulled out a stiff white card. I recognized the writing. It was the same writing I'd seen on envelopes addressed to her mother, the same writing I'd seen on Christmas cards, on recipes, and on grocery lists. It was written in pencil, and there was no mistaking the author.

My dear Brave Rosie,

> *I am so proud of you and all you are doing to take care of dad and the boys. I wish so much to get well and back to you, my precious daughter. I wish I could taste your cornbread and beans. I will love you always.*
> *Your Mama*

81

I cried and kissed the card over and over whispering "Oh, Mama, Mama, Mama." I cried, but it was a different kind of crying. With each tear that fell, a hard piece of gray sadness fell away. I went through the other letters, but none contained another answer. Maybe that was the last time Mama had strength enough to write; maybe someone prevented the letter being mailed. Now it didn't matter. It was a note I would cherish all my life. I put it inside the little Bible I'd been given in Sunday School that winter and kept on my bedside table.

I got dressed in my jeans and the bright red sweater Albert and George had given me for Christmas, and I went downstairs. Mrs. Clausen was making stew. "I'll help you," I told her and began to set the table.

"Rosie, Honey, are you sure you're well?" She clapped her hand to my forehead. "My goodness, you look great, and you feel cool!"

"I found something," I said, and I told her everything.

I went back to school the next morning, and had my work caught up before school was dismissed. Miss Graud told me privately she needed my help with math. It never went as well for her when I wasn't there. Jennifer Olsen somehow created an "I missed you" card and put it on my desk before lunch. Did any of them know the stupid thing I'd done?

There was one person I knew was upset with me, and I wondered if he'd ever be able to understand. I wasn't goofy over Bobby Merritt like half the sixth grade girls were, but I'd always thought he was a good friend. I wondered if we'd ever be friends again.

CHAPTER 29

Annie

I really didn't understand why my parents were having the Thursday night get together, which had now grown to include the Jim Weisels, the Merritts, the Slovens, and all of us. Mrs. Olsen, Billy, and the twins would take care of the store. My mother had a delicious ham cooking in the oven, when we came in from school, and several pots on the counter. My father had laid the special tablecloth on the table and was busy sorting out pieces of china. Edgar was wearing a white shirt and a red tie and a pair of navy dress slacks. A little sports jacket hung in the hallway. He was doing his name card job. I noticed my parents wore "church clothes", too.

"Rosie, come with me," my mother said. "Annie, help your father with the table. I counted the attendees. Our family: 5, the Slovens :4, the Merritts :3, Mr. and Mrs. Jim, 2. Fourteen in all, but then my father said, "Make that 15."

"Is Santa coming for dinner?" I asked my dad.

"He sort of is. No more questions, Annie."

He wasn't quite his usual, relaxed self, and I found myself running to keep up. My mother had made a list, and he sent me to the basement for jars of pickles, jam, and chutney. He counted up how many serving bowls and spoons and knives we needed and set them on the kitchen table. He sent me to check the living room, to be sure it was in order. Mrs. Sloven arrived, and soon the kitchen was being run as if we were serving a battalion. I looked at the food: a huge ham, a turkey, mounds and mounds of mashed potatoes, dressing, gravy, large bowls of corn and green beans, light fluffy dinner rolls, jam, butter. There was a leafy salad and a gelatin one. And pies: apple ones my mother had made, lemon meringue and chocolate from Mrs. Sloven, a sour cream raisin one from Mrs. Jim, and the beautiful peach pie from Mrs. Merritt. This was much more of an occasion than I'd thought.

Now my mother hurried me upstairs to "dress nicely for dinner." On my bed lay a green print dress with a black lace collar. There was also a pair of nylons, my very first, and a garter belt! Wow! And wonder of wonders: a pair of black patent pumps. On my dresser lay a gold and pearl necklace. I worked on my hair, still wet from my shower, but finally my braid fell into place. Mom came up, and twirled it around my head and pinned it down with a small black barrette.

Downstairs, I found Rosie equally elegant in a red dress, her hair pulled back in a pony tail and tied with a large red ribbon. Her skirt was a little shorter and she wore black Mary Janes and white knee socks. She and Edgar were talking brightly to an elderly gentleman, who wore a black judge's robe. The Merritts arrived and I noticed Bobby wore dress slacks and a gray jacket. Mr. and Mrs. Jim came, and all of us were asked by my father to step into the living room and have a seat. Folding chairs from the church stood behind our sofas, and all of us sat where we were told to sit. The Slovens and George and Albert sat on one sofa, and my father, mother, Rosie, Edgar, and I sat on the other.

My father stood and began to speak. "Thank you all so much for coming. On behalf of Herb and Grace and Ellie and myself, I want to welcome all of you who have played such an important role in the lives of our families. We—the Slovens and Clausens—are welcoming by official adoption four very important and beloved children. Our families have agreed to work together to keep these children close to each other. They have proven already to be wonderful family members. Before we begin, Rosie has something she wants to say. Rosie, come on up here."

Surely this wasn't happening. Surely Rosie didn't want to speak in front of that judge and so many other adults. I held my breath, and looked at my dad.

She started to cry, but then by giant effort, she stood up straight, swallowed, and smiled. "I know it was very wrong to go skating alone at night. I did it because, when I was on the ice, I felt like when I was a little girl, and Mama and Dad held onto my hands, and we skated together. When I was on the ice, the terrible sadness went away. I'm very sorry for going, and I'm especially sorry that I broke my promise to Bobby. He found out about it, and I promised him I wouldn't go any more, but I broke my promise. If it hadn't been for Bobby, I would have drowned."

She put her head down for a moment and then continued. "I'm going to be okay now. I found a letter from my mama, and I'm going to be okay." She looked at my parents. "Thank you and Annie for taking Edgar and me."

I was amazed at Rosie's poise and ability to tell the truth and apologize in front of all those people. My mom and dad hugged her, and her brothers hugged her. The Slovens hugged her, and I hugged her finally. As I turned to take a seat on the sofa, Bobby came forward. "I'm so glad you're all right, Rosie. And I'm glad all these Stample kids are my friends." Everyone applauded, and the adoption ceremony for both families proceeded.

It was a wonderful evening. After dinner, all of us who'd been invited to go the state tournament with the Weisels, including Albert and George and Edgar and Rosie and Bobby and I made plans. It was, I decided, as close to a perfect world as I was likely to get.

CHAPTER 30

Rosie

Driving home on Sunday from the State Tournament, I leaned back and closed my eyes and lived again the great time we had all had. Mr. Jim and Mrs. Jim were both good singers and had gotten us started singing halfway to Fargo, and we never let up. Mrs. Jim had brought snacks and the Clausen and Merritt families had sent sweet rolls and small bottles of milk.

Mr. Jim's parents were as gracious as their son and his wife, leading us upstairs to three big bedrooms, one for the Jims, one for Annie and me, and a big, dormitory style room for all four boys. We had time to "tidy up a bit," and then hurried off to the big gymnasium where McFarland would play a team from Belmont, in the western part of the state, at 3:00. What I think I loved the most, even more than McFarland winning the first game was being in the group of people who surrounded me. We yelled, we talked, we laughed, and I was a part of it all. The grayness was gone, and life was beautiful.

After the game we shopped in one of the big department stores. Annie thought we should find matching shirts, since we were now sisters. We found two bold red and white striped knit shirts that would be fun to wear to school. "Let's look in the boy's section for something similar for Edgar," Anne suggested. We found a red striped jersey for him, too.

Mr. Jim's parents met us at a downtown restaurant for dinner before we watched the Neely-Fort Robinson game. How good the food tasted! How good life suddenly was!

After a deep night's sleep, another exciting day began. We watched some of the games; we went to a movie and ate hamburgers for a quick dinner; we watched the McFarland-Neely game. I had never yelled so hard, and Edgar got caught up in the action, too, sitting on the shoulders of Albert, George, and Bobby. McFarland won by one point! We were going to be in the championship game on Saturday evening at 8:00.

Saturday, we stayed at the older Weisel's home, and Mrs. Jim got rested up. All six of us went outside, and we played catch and hide and seek.

We got back to the huge gymnasium way early and found good seats. In spite of our yelling, McFarland lost the game by four points. No one could feel very bad about that. It had been thirty years since McFarland had even won the regionals.

Now driving home, I had relived every happy moment.

It was good to get home, too, to put everything away, and tell the Clausens all about it.

The Slovens came by to pick up Albert and George, who had ridden home with Zack Jones' dad. Mrs. Clausen asked them to stay for supper, and pulled a casserole from the oven. The table was already set. After we'd started eating, Mr. Clausen said, "Greener's came by this morning. This is a spell of good weather, and they want to bury your mama tomorrow about four o'clock. Is that agreeable?"

"Yes," I said. "Now she'll be with Dad."

"She already is," Edgar said.

There was no sadness.

CHAPTER 31

Annie

That summer was hot, and after June, there was little rain. The upstairs was stifling, even with windows open and fans blowing, so Dad hung three hammocks on our big back porch, and Edgar and Rosie and I, dressed in our most threadbare shorts and oldest T-shirts, would grab a sheet and a pillow, and fall asleep there, listening to the crickets chirping. We talked about everything that had happened and danced around dreams for the future, though we never got too far, because first Edgar, and then Rosie would drift off to sleep.

Though school was out, we still had lots of chores. Besides helping at the store, there was continual work in the yard and garden. And after Jennifer Rose Weisel was born, Rosie spent lots of her spare time helping Mrs. Jim. She also endeavored to teach me to do my own laundry, while she did hers and Edgar's. I even learned to iron, though my mother and father still sent theirs to Mrs. Merritt, and my mother continued baking for them.

Still, almost always, there was time in the afternoon for biking or rollerskating or wading in the creek. Life felt good with Rosie and Edgar and Bobby and me sharing the fun.

Sometimes I lay awake wondering what would happen to all of us. In the weeks following their official adoption and the trip to Fargo, Rosie and Edgar began calling my parents Mom and Dad, and I heard Edgar tell a new customer that I was his sister, Annie. And before I knew it, I referred to Edgar as my little brother and Rosie as my sister.

Where would we all be in ten years? It seemed so far in the future—1963. Rosie and I'd be 22 and 23, and Edgar would be nearly 17. What would happen to the Olsens, to Bobby, to George and Albert, to Zack Jones? I usually thought no farther than finishing eighth grade and going to high school. Far, far out was the possibility of college.

Viet Nam was not a country I was familiar with then, and I would have been surprised to learn how it would affect not only my classmates, but all of America.

There was one settled thing in my mind, though. About a week after we got back from the basketball tournament, after Mrs. Stample had been finally laid to rest, Rosie and Edgar had been invited to go with their brothers and the Slovens to Bismarck to see a movie and eat dinner out at a fancy restaurant to celebrate their adoptions. It was a Saturday, and Bobby and I had worked hard all day, but finally at four, we were finished. "Want to get a coke at the drugstore?" Bobby asked.

"I guess."

The drugstore was nearly deserted, and we sat in the corner booth. "It's been quite a year, seventh grade, hasn't it?"

I thought it an odd speech, even for him, but it was true. "Yes, it has."

"I was really mad at you for a long time," he added.

I started to inform him I hadn't been all that thrilled with him either, but then I remembered when he tried to tell me about Rosie, and I hadn't even listened.

"I guess you had a right to be. Are you over it now?"

"Yeah, but I never understood why you were so—so distant to me."

"Well, you and Zack sort of left us out, and kinda went gaga over Mary Lou Minders, and she lied about Evelyn and me not helping her. I was really mad at her."

"Zack and I learned one lesson from her—just because you're pretty doesn't mean you're nice. She was just using us—she wasn't a friend at all."

"I guess everybody figured it out finally." I said. "Anyhow, I'm sorry I didn't listen when you tried to talk to me about Rosie."

He pulled something from his pocket. "I got this for you in Fargo," he said. Inside a small, white, velvety box was a necklace on a silver chain. There were two small white circles hanging from the chain. One said BEST; the other said FRIEND. On the reverse side of BEST, my name was engraved. His was behind FRIEND.

"It's very nice," I managed to say. "Thank you, Bobby."

And then he made one of his grown-up speeches that always startled me.

"You know, who knows how things will turn out? But I just want to be able to count on you, that you'll be my friend, like always. I'm not going to do a lot of boyfriend –girlfriend stuff for a long time, but having a best friend is important to me."

It seemed like a very good arrangement to me, too. I put the necklace around my neck and fastened it. "Thank you," I repeated. "I'm glad we're best friends again."

That night I took the necklace off and noticed the odd-shaped little holes that the chain went through. I was like my mother, needing reading glasses at an early age. The holes puzzled me, and I couldn't focus on them with just my glasses. I went downstairs to my mother's desk, and found her magnifying glass. Then it was easy to see the holes were two tiny hearts.

Most people never saw the necklace as it was usually under my collar, but I had a good feeling knowing it was there, knowing Bobby, maddening and all as he was, was my best friend and I was his.

Edwards Brothers Inc.
Ann Arbor MI. USA
October 5, 2017